MAGIC & MISFITS

STARRY HOLLOW WITCHES, BOOK 13

ANNABEL CHASE

RED PALM PRESS LLC

Copyright © 2020 by Annabel Chase

All rights reserved.

No part of this book may be reproduced in any form or by any electronic or mechanical means, including information storage and retrieval systems, without written permission from the author, except for the use of brief quotations in a book review.

❦ Created with Vellum

CHAPTER ONE

"My knees hurt," I said. I rocked back onto my bottom for a break. Marley and I had been digging and planting along the fence of Rose Cottage for an hour and I'd managed to cut off the circulation to my feet.

Marley cut a sideways glance at me. "You're wearing knee pads and using a garden kneeler."

"Imagine how bad it would be if I weren't."

"I bet they'd hear your complaints all the way back in New Jersey," Marley said, smiling. "This is fun. I like that we're bonding over magic."

"I'd rather bond over a plate of brownies," I said. Even so, I sat back to admire our handiwork. My green thumb was usually more of a dirt brown, but I was making a special effort for this particular project and it showed.

My elderly Yorkshire terrier, Prescott Peabody III, wandered over to sniff one of the plants and promptly lifted his leg.

"I don't think so, mister." I swiped him off the ground before he could sprinkle the plant with his personal brand of rainwater. I set him down on a patch of grass away from the current project. At the rate he moved, he'd age another year before he made his way back over to pollute my plants.

Marley stopped for a drink from her water bottle. "If you want to go inside to make dinner, I'll keep going."

"Do you have any homework?" I asked.

"Finished."

I should've expected that answer. Marley didn't need anyone to remind her. Finishing homework at record speed was as natural as breathing to her.

"How's that charms class going?"

She'd vaguely grumbled about the teacher a few days ago, which I only noticed because Marley rarely complained about anything school-related.

"Fine," she mumbled.

I removed my knee pads and tossed them aside. "Doesn't sound fine."

Marley patted the dirt around the plant with gloved hands, ignoring me.

"Marley Rose, is there anything I should know?"

"I don't like the class. That's all."

"That's like saying Santa doesn't like wine and cheese."

She gave me a pointed look. "He doesn't. He likes milk and cookies. You're the one who tried to convince me he likes wine and cheese."

"Right. Good point." I regarded her closely. The slope of her nose. The sprinkling of freckles on her pale skin. Most importantly, the pulsing muscle in her cheek—the telltale sign that my child was trying to hide her suffering. "Sweetheart, if there's an issue, I want to know about it. Keeping it to yourself will only make it seem worse."

Marley chewed her lip. "I can handle it on my own."

"There's a difference between handle and endure. From the look on your face, I'd say you're enduring."

She removed her gloves and clutched them in her lap. "I'm having trouble with a couple witches in the class."

I peered at her, my tension rising. "What kind of trouble?"

"They keep playing magical pranks on me when the teacher isn't looking and Mrs. Croft-Merryman thinks I'm to blame."

"Why are they picking on you? I thought you were getting along really well with the others."

Her eyes were downcast. "Because they overheard their parents talking about our rift with Aunt Hyacinth. I guess that means it's open season on me now."

My mouth dropped open. "You can't be serious. How on earth do they know what happened?"

"I don't know that they do, only that you and Aunt Hyacinth aren't on speaking terms and that we're no longer welcome at Thornhold."

I knew we shouldn't have gone out for Sunday dinner last week. Word must've spread that we weren't partaking in the weekly family dinners and made other residents curious as to why. Or, even worse, Aunt Hyacinth was letting everyone know where we stood in order to ostracize us.

"Why didn't you tell me?" I demanded. Marley and I had always enjoyed a close relationship. It wasn't like her to keep things from me.

"Because I don't want you to go Jersey on anybody. It'll only make things worse."

I felt awful. The fallout with Aunt Hyacinth was bad enough on the home front. Now it was spilling over into Marley's academic life.

"I'm so sorry, Marley. I should've realized how my actions might affect you."

"I don't blame you," she said matter-of-factly. "I blame Aunt Hyacinth for being greedy and unreasonable."

My chest ached. I hated to see my daughter reaping what

I had sown when I refused to pass our ancestor Ivy's incredible power to my aunt. "You don't think I've been too stubborn?"

"No way. She used me, Mom. She only gave me Ivy's wand to see whether I could access the magic. It was cunning and manipulative."

That described Aunt Hyacinth to a T. Still, I didn't want Marley to think she didn't matter. "I'm sure part of her wanted you to have something special, to pass on a family heirloom to the next generation."

"You don't have to sugarcoat it, Mom. She wanted Ivy's power for herself. That was her only motivation." Marley put her gloves back on. "The truth is she doesn't deserve us in her life."

"What kind of pranks have the witches been pulling?" My blood began to boil at the thought of those wretched girls upsetting my sweet daughter.

"Nothing complicated. They're not talented enough for that." She allowed herself a small smile. "They did a spell that erased my homework and another one that made me hiccup so much that Mrs. Croft-Merryman asked me to leave class."

In a show of sympathy, PP3 climbed onto Marley's lap and licked her arm.

"And you haven't told anyone at school?" I asked, knowing what the answer would be.

"It'll only make them dislike me more." Her lower lip jutted out. "The worst part is that I thought they liked me, but it turns out they only tolerated me because of our family connection."

"Then better to know the truth," I said. "You want genuine friendships, not a bunch of sycophants."

Marley smiled. "Good job on the fifty-cent word."

"Hey, I think that one's at least a dollar when you take

inflation into account." I blew out a breath. "Oh, Marley. I hate that you're dealing with this."

She shrugged, her expression far too solemn for a girl of her age. "We all have to grow up eventually."

"Really? That's news to me. I plan to stay immature forever."

We were so intent on our conversation that we failed to notice Florian's arrival until he was just outside the white picket fence.

"Is there a famine in the forecast?" my cousin asked, surveying our endeavor.

"We're not planting potatoes," I said, "and I don't think you'd survive on these."

"Well, they smell good, whatever they are," Florian said.

I pointed to the plant directly in front of me. "This is basil."

The wizard peered over the fence. "Yes, I recognize that one. Why are you growing it here instead of in the herb garden?"

"Because it's to protect the cottage from negative energy," I said.

"And this is black cohosh," Marley added, pointing to her row, "to protect against a magical attack."

Florian's brow furrowed as he examined the plants. "All this because you had a tiff with Mother?"

"It's more than a tiff, Florian," I said. "We're officially on the outs."

He motioned to the proverbial line in the sand. "And you really think this is necessary?"

"Better safe than sorry." I rose to my feet and dusted off my knees. "You're always welcome, of course. Want to come inside? I have beer."

He entered through the gate. "I'm not sure it's wise. I

might get eaten by a carnivorous plant when I'm not looking."

"Don't be ridiculous," Marley said. "The only man-eater in this cottage is Mom."

I jerked my head toward her, feeling indignant. "Hey! Uncalled for."

Marley appeared unapologetic and carried on planting. "We don't really have time for beer. We need to get these finished by sundown."

Florian snorted. "Or what? Mother will launch an attack?"

I looked him directly in the eye. "Honestly, I have no idea what she'll do at this point. I have something she wants and we both know she won't leave me alone until she gets it."

Florian pursed his lips. "I don't like this, Ember. Family squabbles are one thing, but this…" He nudged a plant with his toe. "This is next level."

"Don't blame me," I said. "She's the one who disinvited us from Sunday dinners."

Florian balked. "She did? She told me you were both feeling under the weather."

"She lied," I said simply. "Simon delivered the message on her behalf. Believe me, he wasn't thrilled with his role as the middle man."

Florian dragged a hand through his white-blond hair. "I didn't realize she'd officially thrown down the gauntlet. I'm sorry."

"It's fine," I said. "Like I told you, you're always welcome here."

"I appreciate that." He paused. "Do Linnea and Aster know?"

"I haven't given them the particulars, no."

"You should. Don't let Mother get ahead of you or you'll

be inundated with damage control and little else. You want to be proactive in this situation, not reactive."

"Thanks for the tip." I wiped my brow with a gloved hand. "Ready for a break, Marley? I wouldn't object to an iced tea."

Marley popped up from the ground. "I'll get it." She skipped into the cottage.

I waited until the door closed to speak again. "She's having trouble at school. Word has spread about our rift with your mother and a few witches are giving Marley a hard time."

Florian's nostrils flared. "I'll have their names, please."

"No, we'll handle it. Thanks, though."

"It isn't right."

"Of course not, but your mother's treatment of us sets the tone for others, whether we agree with it or not. Marley's putting on a brave face, but I know it can't be easy. She was finally settled and now this."

"Let me know if there's anything I can do," he said. "I hate the thought of anyone causing problems for Marley."

"Believe me, I feel the same."

He motioned to the ground between us. "I can understand you feeling vulnerable, especially living so close to Thornhold, but I don't think you need all this defense against the dark arts. She might play her power games and punish you for not towing the line, but I can't picture her using magic to hurt either of you."

"Then you haven't seen the same look in her eye that I have. She's angry, Florian. She wants Ivy's power and she's furious that I have it."

Florian eyed me closely. "And why is that, exactly?"

"It was an accident. I didn't intend to absorb all her magic."

He shook his head. "No, I mean why do you refuse to let it go? If you didn't intend to take it, then why keep it?"

My eyes popped. "And give it to your mother, already the most powerful witch in Starry Hollow? Gee, I don't know. Maybe because I dislike the idea of all the power being concentrated in one individual."

"Now you sound like Sheriff Nash. I think his ideas have rubbed off on you."

"Do you seriously think I should let her have it?" I asked, surprised. Florian was a mama's boy, but still. I didn't expect him to take her side. Not with this.

"She has the same claim to it that you do," Florian said. "So do I, for that matter. We're all descendants of Ivy Rose."

"Except possession is nine-tenths of the law." I had no idea what that meant, but I'd watched enough episodes of Law & Order to recognize the phrase.

"What law?" Florian asked. "You know your human laws don't apply here."

"Even if I could pass it on, I don't know how it would work. I didn't access Ivy's magic on purpose, so I certainly don't know how to hand it off to someone else."

Florian offered a vague smile. "Oh, I don't think you'd have to worry about the logistics. If you were willing to part with it, Mother would find a way. She's nothing if not persistent."

I glanced toward the sprawling home of Hyacinth Rose-Muldoon in the distance. "That's exactly what I'm afraid of."

CHAPTER TWO

I PAGED THROUGH THE GRIMOIRE, looking for a spell that might help Marley. I didn't want to stoop to the level of her wicked classmates, but I hoped to find something that would put a permanent end to their bullying without getting other adults involved. The last thing Marley wanted was to draw attention to herself. The introvert in her would fall to pieces.

"Making them itch probably isn't a solution," I mused. Unless I made them itch until they swore never to bother Marley again. Hmm. Probably too extreme. I flipped the page over and continued my search.

I spotted a spell to make the soles of their shoes slippery. That might work to humiliate them, as well as provide entertainment for fans of physical comedy. A win-win. I reviewed the instructions and didn't notice anything out of Marley's depth. I contemplated whether I should encourage retaliation. The adult in me knew it wasn't the right way to handle it, but the immature part of me wanted to see these opportunistic witches learn a lesson, preferably on their butts in the middle of a crowded corridor.

PP3 stood and growled at the door.

"Who needs a protective ward when I have you?" I asked, patting the dog on the head as I headed to answer the door. The knock came just as I grabbed the handle to open it.

Raoul stood on the doorstep accompanied by a strange creature with wings too small for its portly body. His skin had a pinkish hue and his eyes were small and dark.

"You're using the front door?" I asked. "Is the kitchen window broken?"

Raoul ignored me. *I'd like you to meet my new friend, Arnold Palmer.*

"Like the drink that's half iced tea and half lemonade?" I asked.

The raccoon shook his head.

"Oh, like the golfer?"

The raccoon looked at me askance. *Like the pink fairy armadillo.*

Ah, so that's what he was. "Nice to meet you, Mr. Palmer," I said.

Arnold Palmer is one word, Raoul said.

"No, it's not. It's two."

No, it's like CindyLou or MaryJo, Raoul countered. *One.*

"A-Pa?" I offered.

Raoul glowered at me. *Just no.*

I opened the door and stepped aside. "Come on in. What can I do for you?"

Arnold Palmer needs our help, Raoul said. *I told him you're a mighty witch.*

"I'm mighty tired is what I am, but sure. What seems to be the trouble?" I held up a finger. "Hold on. It's probably best not to leave the translation to Raoul."

What's wrong with my translations?

My hands landed on my hips. "Go on then. Tell me what your friend needs."

An extra-large pizza with pepperoni and sausage for starters.

Without that, it's hard for him to form the right words. Melted cheese loosens the tongue.

"That's what I figured." I crossed the room to the altar where my Book of Shadows rested. There was a spell I'd copied for future use that would come in handy now.

Raoul tugged on my pant leg. *What are you doing? How can you help him before you hear his problem?*

"I'm going to cast a spell so that I can hear his problem directly and not through you." I kept my focus on the page. "I need a few herbs from the garden. Can I trust you to collect them without eating any?"

Raoul pulled a face. *Herbs? Yeah, I think you can trust me.*

"I need basil, thyme, grapeseed oil, and sandalwood chips. I'll get the oil and a glass jar and you can get the rest."

Raoul scurried out of the cottage and I motioned for Arnold Palmer to follow me into the kitchen. I grabbed the items from the pantry and poured the oil into the base of the jar. Once Raoul returned with the rest, I added the ingredients to the jar and mixed them in a clockwise direction.

"You awaken. You speak. We listen," I chanted as I stirred.

I left the mixture to rest a moment and went to retrieve a collar and a small vial. I added some of the mixture to the vial and stored the rest in a container.

Smells good enough to eat, Raoul said.

I hooked the vial onto the collar and bent down to address Arnold Palmer. "I'm going to attach this to a collar around your neck. As long as you're wearing it, you'll be able to communicate with anyone you choose."

The collar has shamrocks on it, Raoul said. *Did you steal it from a sadistic leprechaun?*

"No, it was for PP3 to wear on St. Patrick's Day," I said.

Raoul shook his head. *Humans.*

I smiled at the pink fairy armadillo. "Why don't you tell me why you're here?"

"Good day, miss. It's a pleasure to meet you."

Why can't I have one of those so everyone can hear me? Raoul asked.

Because then everyone could hear you.

You're depriving the world of the voice of a generation.

Swap 'depriving' for 'saving.'

"I do so appreciate your assistance with this delicate matter," Arnold Palmer continued. "It's a relief to find someone with your skills in Starry Hollow willing to take on new clients."

"You need magic?"

"No, I need someone with a discerning eye."

I looked at Raoul askance. *And you brought him to me?*

He doesn't need someone to dress him.

"How delicate are we talking?" I asked.

The pink fairy armadillo's stomach brushed against the floor, his gossamer wings too weak to lift his portly body completely into the air.

"You see, I was formerly the familiar of a witch named Heloise Gumtree."

"Is she in my coven?" I didn't recall anyone with a pink fairy armadillo companion. I would have remembered that strange pairing. Raoul and I were the lone misfits. Even Bonkers was part cat.

"No, no. Heloise and I lived in a lovely coastal town in Devon."

"Pennsylvania?"

"England, miss."

I scratched my head. "And how did you end up here?"

Arnold Palmer seemed to tire of trying to fly and settled on the floor at my feet. "I answered an advertisement on the interwebs."

There's a service that matches witches and familiars, Raoul added.

"Won't they help you connect with a witch?" I asked. That seemed to be the whole point of the service.

"According to the reviews, they have a tendency to rush you into a match in order to collect their commission," he said. "I have no intention of rushing into such a momentous decision. There's far too much at stake."

I wouldn't trust their opinion either, Raoul said. *I bet they'd lie about someone's background just to make the match, like my stockbroker.*

I shot the raccoon a quizzical look. "You have a stockbroker?"

Not anymore.

I returned my attention to Arnold Palmer. "Why use the service at all?"

"Because I believe the suggestions are genuine and the questionnaire I completed was thorough, but I'm skeptical of their interpretation of the results. I'd like more information before I render a decision."

"So what do you want from me?" I asked.

"I would like my prospects vetted by an independent third party," he said. "I have a checklist of wants and needs to guide you."

"Don't we all?" I muttered.

"I'd like to put my considerable talents to good use and give input into the garden. I'd also like someone who appreciates my cooking."

Raoul perked up at the mention of cooking. *I wouldn't mind having a familiar of my own. Maybe he can be my companion.*

I smiled at the visitor. "It sounds like you're creating a wish list for a second marriage."

"It's not too far off, I suppose. Heloise wasn't exactly the nicest witch in the world, you see, and I would prefer a more positive experience this time around."

I eyed Raoul. *And you chose me to help? Why?* I was hardly the best judge of good relationships.

Because he's willing to pay. Why else?

"I'd like it to be the best of all possible matches, the kind that you have with Raoul," Arnold Palmer said.

I cut a quick glance at the raccoon. Did we have the best of all possible matches? It could definitely be worse.

"What happened to Heloise?" I asked. "Someone threw a bucket of water on her and she melted?"

Arnold Palmer sniffed. "As though such a thing were possible. No, a broomstick mishap. She was flying over the harbor in Torbay as a storm rolled in. The wind knocked her from her broom and she plunged into the sea and drowned."

I grimaced. "That's terrible. I'm so sorry."

"I'm only grateful I wasn't with her at the time," the pink fairy armadillo said. "I'd offered to accompany her, but she refused. I believe she said—'what need have I for a useless sidekick who's too fat to fly solo?'"

"Sounds like she was a real charmer," I said.

"Hence my trepidation. I want to choose wisely, Miss Rose, now that I have the option."

"And you've already narrowed down the field?"

He nodded. "The agency sent me three names in Starry Hollow, which is why I've come here first. I'm hopeful that you can vet all three."

"What happens if none of them make the cut?" I asked.

Arnold Palmer lowered his head. "I fear I haven't been willing to contemplate that possibility. Starry Hollow seems like a charming town and I'd love to settle here. Find a place where I feel at home."

"I don't want to mislead you. I'm not a matchmaker or a detective," I protested.

You're sort of a detective, Raoul said. *Like a private investiga-*

tor, only your investigation report ends up printed in the newspaper.

Arnold Palmer's eyes brimmed with tears. "Apologies, Miss Rose. I was under the impression that this was your speciality."

Oh gods, I couldn't stand here and watch a pink fairy armadillo cry. I wasn't a monster.

"I can do it," I said.

A fat tear dropped from his eye and splashed on the floor. "Are you certain?"

"Absolutely. One hundred percent. No charge."

Raoul's head jerked toward me. *No charge? Have you lost your mind? Is this a sign of early menopause?*

Raoul might've been unhappy, but Arnold Palmer was elated. "Thank you, miss. This is wonderful news. Truly." He produced a scrap of paper out of thin air. "Here's the list. They're all local. I haven't met them yet. I'd rather not until I know that I want to."

"Understood." I glanced at the names—Violet Bay-Moonstone, Laurel Honeywell, and Lavender Soap. "Um, Arnold Palmer, I think you may have mixed up your grocery list with this one."

"No, I'm afraid that last name is accurate."

Well, that was unfortunate.

Do you know any of them? Raoul asked.

I don't recognize the names.

They must be in the coven.

Not necessarily, but I'll see what I can find out. If there was a reason they didn't mix with everybody else, better to know now.

"I am forever indebted to you, Miss Rose," the armadillo said.

I leaned down to pat his head. "Don't put the cart in front

of the horse. Be forever indebted to me after I've found your perfect match."

CHAPTER THREE

I POKED my head into the *Vox Populi* office to make sure the coast was clear before fully entering.

"Yes, this is where you work," Bentley said. "Well done."

I glared at the elf as I made my way to the neighboring desk. "I just wanted to make sure my aunt wasn't paying us a visit." As the owner of the newspaper, Aunt Hyacinth occasionally popped in unexpectedly.

"Why? Are you in trouble?" The elf sounded far too delighted by the prospect.

The news of our rift hadn't yet made it to the newspaper. How ironic.

"None of your business," I said. I twisted to see whether the door to Alec's office was open. As the editor-in-chief, the vampire was in the unfortunate position of being both my boss and my boyfriend.

"She's not in there," Bentley said, noticing me. "Neither is he, for that matter."

"Has he been here at all today?" I asked.

Bentley frowned. "Shouldn't you know that? I thought you two were joined at the lip."

"It's the hip," I corrected him.

He turned back to his computer screen. "Not in your case."

I smiled to myself, remembering our most recent lip lock. Alec and I did have amazing chemistry. Unfortunately, chemistry wasn't enough to overcome some of the issues we'd been trying in vain to address. And my problem with Aunt Hyacinth only served to increase the tension between us. Alec didn't want to be stuck in the middle. Aunt Hyacinth was his boss and their working relationship began long before I arrived on the scene in Starry Hollow.

"Where's Tanya?" I asked.

"Hair appointment. She'll be in shortly."

"What are you working on?" I asked, shoving aside all thoughts of my aunt. I needed something else to focus on or I'd go nuts.

Bentley tapped on his keyboard, ignoring my question.

I leaned over to look at the file on his desk and my heart skipped a beat. "Roy Nash? You're still working on this?"

Bentley had recently shared his intention to investigate cold cases so he could write articles about them and he planned to start with the unsolved murder of Sheriff Nash's father.

"I got sidetracked by other projects but decided to really dig in."

"You should talk to Sheriff Nash," I said. "Compare notes."

Bentley gave me a skeptical look. "I thought you were worried it would upset him."

"I've changed my mind. He's been working on the case on the side over the years. He might appreciate the extra set of eyes."

Bentley perked up. "Are you serious? Do you think he'll mind sharing?"

"The only way to find out is to ask."

The elf regarded me with interest. "Why don't you ask him for me?"

"Why me?"

He rolled his eyes. "Are you really going to ask that? You know why."

"The sheriff isn't more likely to..." Oh, who was I kidding? "Fine, I'll talk to him for you."

"See if he'll give you his notes," Bentley said. "No reason to reinvent the wheel."

The door opened and Alec entered the office. The vampire looked exceptionally handsome in a light grey suit and crisp white shirt.

"We're working hard, boss," I announced, making a show of pounding the keys.

He ignored my exaggerated display. "Are you available for dinner this evening?"

"With you? Let me check my calendar." I glanced at my phone. "I've got a hot date with a pink fairy armadillo but otherwise I'm totally free."

"Excellent. Does seven o'clock suit you?"

"I like to eat dinner, too," Bentley said to no one in particular.

"Your place or mine?" I frowned. "Make that yours. I haven't cleaned Bonkers' litter box."

"How about the Lighthouse instead?" he asked.

"Oh. What's the occasion?" It wasn't a birthday or an anniversary.

He rested his hands on top of my computer. "Does there need to be an occasion to dine with you somewhere with exceptional food?"

"No, but we've gotten in the habit of eating at home," I said. "I thought there might be a reason."

He leaned over and kissed the top of my head. "I'll pick you up at seven."

"Okay. I'll wear something provocative enough to make the staff wonder if you're out with a hooker."

Bentley strangled a laugh.

"Please don't," Alec said. "What are you working on now?"

"The vandalism article," I said.

"Have you even started that yet?" Bentley asked.

"I named the file," I said, pointing to my computer screen. "That counts."

Bentley scowled.

"What are you working on, Bentley?" Alec asked.

The elf was taken off-guard. "Oh, uh. The high school is getting a new roof."

"Fascinating," Alec said. He continued to his office at the back of the room.

"Why didn't you tell him about the cold case?" I asked.

"Do you really think he'd want me helping the sheriff? You know better than anyone they don't get along."

"Technically, you're not helping the sheriff. Your goal is the article."

Bentley resumed typing. "Still, I'm not going to risk Alec telling me to abandon it."

"I have to admit, your thing is more interesting than mine. Vandals painting lewd comments on Muse Fountain isn't very exciting."

"I'd be happy to trade with you."

"Not today, Satan." I managed to sift through my notes and write the entire first paragraph before my phone alarm sounded.

Bentley smirked. "End of the day already?"

"Hardly. I've got a magical sergeant waiting for me in the woods."

"Sounds kinky. Does Alec know?"

I closed the document and grabbed my purse. "I'll get the information from Sheriff Nash before I come back."

"And I suppose you'll stop at the Caffeinated Cauldron, too."

"And for lunch," I added, smiling. "A girl's got to eat."

Bentley shook his head, scowling. "Must be nice to be you."

I peered out the window for any sign of Marigold. The witch was never late, but I'd waited in the woods behind the cottage for twenty minutes before giving up and returning home. There was no answer to my calls or texts either, which was unusual. Marigold was a stickler for everything, including punctuality. The last time I was late to a lesson, she made me form a psychic link with a toad from the nearby pond and see if I could persuade it to stop eating flies. Naturally, the toad had no interest in abstaining and thought I was lunatic. You haven't been properly humiliated until an ugly toad has given you side-eye. Marigold took fiendish pleasure in watching me struggle. Pretty sure she even recorded the endeavor on her phone, although she swore up and down she did no such thing.

I considered calling the local healers' offices to see whether she'd been brought in unconscious. As I was about to turn away from the window when I observed a seagull swoop down and perch on the fencepost. Although the birds were a staple at the beach, we rarely had them turn up at the cottage. Upon closer scrutiny, I realized the seagull clutched something in its beak and I went out to investigate.

The moment the door cracked open, the bird dropped the object and flew away. I rushed forward to grab the item before the wind took it. I plucked the tightly folded paper from between two blades of grass and opened it as I returned to the cottage. I immediately recognized Marigold's neat and precise handwriting. That saved me a bunch of frantic phone calls, at least.

My dearest Ember,

It pains me to tell you this, but I'm afraid that I am unable to continue

our lessons as planned. Hyacinth has decided that you require no further

education on the subject of magic. Henceforth, all future lessons are cancelled.

No further education? The timing couldn't have been worse. As far as I was concerned, my recent influx of power made my lessons a necessity more than ever. As much as I complained, I found the army of coven tutors indispensable when it came to exploring and developing my skills.

I leaned against the door and sighed. Aunt Hyacinth was determined to punish me in every possible way, it seemed. It was to her disadvantage, though. With Ivy's power, I could cause mass destruction if I wasn't careful. The Rose name would be dragged through the mud all over again. My aunt was more terrified of a besmirched reputation than nuclear war.

PP3 lifted his head from his curled-up position on the sofa, as though sensing my disappointment.

"It's okay, buddy," I said. "It's not like I ever wanted those lessons. Aunt Hyacinth forced them on me." I still had my own resources, including Ivy's Book of Shadows and grimoire, as well as Artemis. And I was certain my cousins would still offer magical help if I needed it. They'd just want to do it behind their mother's back. Florian loved us, but he loved his bottomless bank account more, I suspected.

My gaze fell upon the dining table where Hazel and I often held our runecraft lessons. No more Big Book of Scribbles. At least there was a silver lining.

I tucked the note in my pocket. Without lessons, I'd have more time to commit to Marley and Alec, as well as my job. It was a good thing...wasn't it?

I decided to take advantage of my unexpected freedom and head to the sheriff's office now to talk to Sheriff Nash about his father's case. That would leave me plenty of time to make dinner for Marley and get ready for my evening out with Alec. I liked the idea of Bentley owing me a favor, if only because it would irk the elf to no end to have that hanging over his pointy ears.

I greeted the receptionist with a friendly smile and kept walking. Everybody knew me in the sheriff's office and didn't seem bothered by my presence. Deputy Bolan was the only one who would give me a hard time about stopping to see the sheriff without an appointment. To be fair, the cantankerous leprechaun would give me a hard time about handing him a winning lottery ticket.

My eyes widened at the sight of a curvaceous werewolf perched on the edge of the sheriff's desk. With her plump lips and sandy-colored hair, she looked more like a swimsuit model than a deputy.

"Sorry, I didn't mean to interrupt a meeting."

His guest slid off the desk and turned to face me.

"Ember Rose, I'd like you to meet my new deputy, Valentina Pitt." He looked at his companion. "Ember is a reporter for the local newspaper, so you can expect to see a great deal of her."

Deputy Pitt's gaze flicked over me. "I'll make a note of it. Wouldn't want to arrest her for trespassing."

"No, you definitely don't want to do that. Her aunt is Hyacinth Rose-Muldoon. If you don't recognize that name already, then you will. Trust me."

I ignored the remark about my aunt. She was the last paranormal I wanted to discuss right now.

"What happened to Bolan?" I asked in an effort to steer the conversation away from my relations.

"Nothing happened to him," the sheriff said. "We've been needing an extra pair of handcuffs for quite some time and Deputy Pitt will fill that role nicely."

I'll bet. She'd fill a bikini nicely, too, although I hoped to never see it.

I offered a polite smile and shook her hand. "It's nice to meet you, Deputy."

"You, too." Her large hazel eyes were slanted like a cat's and her lashes were so thick that she didn't need mascara. Some women had all the luck.

"Did you two already know each other?" I asked. I didn't recall the sheriff ever mentioning the name Valentina or Pitt.

"No," she said. "I moved here a few months ago from Florida."

"What brought you here?" I asked.

"I'd visited here with my Nana on vacation and fell in love. Decided when the time came, I'd up sticks and find a place here."

"And I guess the time came," I said.

"Well, that's what happens when you end a relationship." She flashed a smile that didn't quite reach her expressive eyes. "Like they say, when you close one door, another door opens."

I nodded. "They do say that, don't they?" I shifted my attention to the sheriff. "Could we talk in private for a minute?"

"Don't mind me. I'm heading out anyway," Deputy Pitt

said. "Deputy Bolan offered to show me the downtown area. He wants me to know the most likely places for traffic violations."

"When you find out, would you share them with me so I can avoid them?"

The deputy laughed. "Sure thing. It was nice meeting you." Deputy Pitt's gaze drifted to the sheriff and she lowered her lashes. "See you later, boss." She sauntered out of the office, swaying her ample hips with each step.

"Hmm," I said, once she was gone.

"How am I meant to interpret that?" Sheriff Nash asked good-naturedly.

I gave him an innocent look. "Interpret what?"

"Unlike Alec Hale, I'm not the type to take up with one of my employees," he said. "It's unprofessional."

"I guess that makes me unprofessional, too."

The sheriff motioned for me to sit. "What brings you in, Rose?"

"A project." I drew a deep breath and prayed I didn't upset him. "Bentley has taken it upon himself to investigate a cold case so he can write a story about it."

Sheriff Nash nodded approvingly. "That takes initiative."

"Well, he says it's because Alec gives me all the best stories, but whatever." I rubbed my hands on my thighs, feeling nervous. "Anyhoo, the case he wants to revisit is your dad's."

My revelation was met with silence. I watched his face for any sign of displeasure.

"Is that so?" he finally asked, keeping his expression neutral.

Sweet baby Elvis, why were ruggedly handsome faces so difficult to read?

"You know Bentley. He's desperate to impress and he thinks solving a case like this will be the story of the year."

"I guess it would be," the sheriff said. "A high-profile, unsolved murder of a local husband and father. The sheriff's father, no less."

"I know it's a sensitive subject for you, and I want to know if you have any objections. If you do, Bentley will back off." And by back off, I meant I would steal his file and hide it somewhere the elf would never find it.

The sheriff licked his lips, appearing to consider whether he did, in fact, harbor any objections to a random elf ripping open an old wound. "I don't mind, Rose. In fact, I'll even share my notes with him."

My breath caught in my throat. "You will?"

"Sure. Truth is, I'll be impressed if he solves a case I haven't been able to solve myself."

"You don't have a murder board, do you?" I asked.

He eyed me curiously. "I'm a sheriff, Rose. Why would I have a board of paranormals I want to murder?"

"No, no. Not like that. One of those big whiteboards with tangled string and newspaper clippings that show how aliens murdered your father? Whenever you look at it, you get crazy eyes." I widened my eyes dangerously close to popping them out of their sockets to demonstrate my version of crazy eyes.

He chuckled. "No, Rose. I'll leave crazy eyes to those who are actually nuts."

"This is great, thanks. Bentley will be thrilled."

He gave me a curious look. "Just Bentley?"

"Well, I'm sure I'll end up helping a little. The poor guy can't seem to do anything without me." Whether he liked it or not.

His smile faded. "Everything good with you, Rose? You seem a little off."

I debated whether to tell him about my issue with Aunt

Hyacinth. He'd likely give me an I-told-you-so look with those soulful brown eyes. No thanks.

"Everything's peachy keen, jellybean." I resumed a standing position. "I'll share the good news with Bentley."

"Tell him thank you for me. I'm grateful that someone else is taking an interest in the case."

"And I'm grateful to you for saving me from listening to him moan and complain about his assignments. This will tide him over for weeks." Maybe even months if I was lucky.

Sheriff Nash studied me intently. "You sure you're okay? I'm getting serious distress signals."

I glanced down at my top. "That's only because I neglected to put on my bra this morning."

He stifled a laugh. "Now I need to keep my eyes on the desk until you leave."

"Yes, you've enjoyed quite an eyeful of curves today already, haven't you?" I rose from the chair and held my purse against my chest. "Let me know when you have the notes and I'll get them from you."

"Only if you're fully dressed. Wouldn't want to cause any trouble between you and Hale."

"No, definitely not."

Aunt Hyacinth was causing more than enough trouble for me at the moment. There was no reason to add my boyfriend to the list.

CHAPTER FOUR

"You look pretty, Mom," Marley said from her place on the sofa. She had a book spread across her lap and PP3 curled up beside her. Bonkers was making use of the scratching post while Raoul raided the pantry for snacks.

"Thanks. We haven't been out to dinner recently, so I thought I'd make an extra effort to look nice." I backed away from the window where my nose had basically been pressed against the glass for the past fifteen minutes. He was late and I'd started to worry that I'd receive a similar note from Alec like the one I'd received from Marigold.

"Well, mission accomplished," she said. "I'm glad he's taking you out. It'll take your mind off your lessons."

"Or lack thereof," I said. Marley had been appalled when I told her about Marigold's note.

Alec's limo pulled up in front of the cottage and butterflies rushed around my stomach. I didn't know why I felt anxious about our date. We'd eaten out together plenty of times.

"Have fun," Marley said

"Are you sure you're okay being here alone?" I asked.

Marley spared a glance over her shoulder. "Just go and enjoy yourself. This cottage is warded to the max now, remember? Forget Aunt Hyacinth. Nobody could get in here unless we want them to."

I hadn't anticipated that a byproduct of protecting ourselves from my aunt would be a boost to Marley's confidence.

I'll take it, I thought.

I ducked out of the cottage before Alec could come to the door. No need to rouse PP3. He'd only need to go outside to pee again.

The limo door was open so I slid into the backseat. Alec sat at the far end, still wearing his light grey suit. Normally the vampire changed before going out to dinner. He was fastidious about his clothes, and office attire was not interchangeable with dinner attire, never mind they were both tailored suits. I mean, I'd gone to the trouble of putting on a bra.

The driver closed my door and I turned to smile at him. "Busy day?"

"Unfortunately. My agent isn't in love with the chapters I sent her. She thinks I should add more humor."

"Humor isn't exactly your trademark." I reached across the seat to pat his thigh and noticed him flinch. "Is something wrong?"

The vampire forced a smile, showing off his fangs. "No. I'm starving and looking forward to a nice meal. That's all." He wiggled his fingers, indicating for me to move closer.

I slid across the seat to nestle in the crook of his arm. "Aunt Hyacinth cancelled all my tutors. No more magic lessons."

He kissed the top of my head. "I'm sorry. She has a vindictive side, I'm afraid."

"Does she think I'm going to do what she wants by

bullying me?" I craned my neck to look at him. "Has she met me? Trying to force my hand will only make me do the opposite."

"She's bitter and angry and lashing out," he said, stroking my hair. "This, too, shall pass."

"I hope it passes before too long. She's like an angry toddler who thinks I stole her doll."

"I'm sure you can supplement your lessons. There must be others who can step into their shoes."

"There are very few coven members willing to get on the wrong side of my aunt. I've been doing my own research, though. Between Marley and me, we'll make sure I don't have a magical meltdown."

The driver dropped us off in front of the restaurant and Alec took my arm to escort me to the elevator. We rode to the top of the building in silence. Despite his pleasant tone, something seemed off, but I couldn't quite put my finger on it. Although he said and did all the right things, the vampire didn't seem entirely himself.

The hostess sat us at a reserved table for two with a sweeping view of both the town and the ocean. It was also spaced far enough apart from the other tables to offer an added bit of privacy. I wondered whether he'd requested a private table.

Alec ordered a bottle of Malbec and a glass of Scotch before his bottom hit the chair. The vampire seemed... nervous. Alec Hale was never nervous.

"Scotch?" I queried.

He offered an easygoing smile. "Why not?"

Something was definitely amiss.

I ignored the menu and focused on him. I already knew what I wanted to order anyway.

"Marley's having trouble with some of her classmates," I said.

He peered at me over the top of the menu. "What kind of trouble?"

"They must've heard about Aunt Hyacinth shunning us and Marley's suddenly become prey for the academy's apex predators."

"They probably resented her position of prestige before and now they have the opportunity to express it."

"Marley didn't ask to be a Rose and she certainly doesn't flaunt it. Their behavior says more about them than her."

"I agree." He returned his attention to the menu and it felt as though he'd erected a wall.

The server returned with our drinks and took our order. I opted for the blackened swordfish with sweet potato hash and Alec chose steak.

"A creature of habit," I said, smiling. When he failed to return the smile, a knot formed in my stomach. The air between us crackled with tension and I was at a loss as to the reason. It wasn't as though my refusal to bow to my aunt's wishes impacted Alec. His position in town was rock solid.

Alec summoned the server back to the table. "We'll take a bottle of champagne, too, please. Two flutes."

I raised my brow. "Are we drinking all our calories tonight?"

As I watched Alec absently pat his jacket pocket, a thought seized me.

Was he going to propose?

That would explain the fancy dinner and his display of nerves. Maybe it was his attempt to alleviate the friction with my aunt. A wedding would trump everything else, wouldn't it?

I finished an entire glass of wine in silence. Finally, I couldn't take the suspense anymore.

"Spill it, Alec," I demanded.

The vampire's expression revealed nothing. "I don't know what you mean."

"Something's going on. I can feel it. Please tell me."

"Why don't we wait for the champagne?"

Oh gods. There *was* something going on. If he did get down on one knee, what would I say? Our relationship hadn't exactly been smooth sailing. Could I marry someone who refused to work on improving the relationship? What kind of message would that send to Marley? That her mother didn't feel she deserved more out of a relationship and was willing to settle?

My head continued to buzz with competing thoughts and emotions. By the time the server arrived with the bottle and flutes, I felt ready to be sick. She popped the cork and filled both flutes. I inspected my glass to make sure there was no ring at the bottom.

Once the server departed, Alec sighed and glanced out the window at the twinkling lights of Starry Hollow. "I generally have the luxury of doing what I want, when I want, but there are rare occasions when that simply isn't possible."

Was he concerned with giving up his freedom if we got married? It made sense. He was a vampire who'd been on his own for longer than I'd been alive. It would an adjustment for both of us.

"You're not an island, Alec. Sometimes you have to compromise."

He shook his head sadly. "If only it were a compromise."

I sucked down the flute of champagne as a feeling of dread washed over me. If this was a marriage proposal, it wasn't a particularly good one.

"That's cryptic," I said. "Can you say that in a language I understand?"

He turned away from the window and met my gaze. "I'm afraid I have to let you go."

Okay. Definitely not the expected start to a marriage proposal. "Let me go?"

He cleared his throat. "From *Vox Populi*. Hyacinth has insisted that I terminate your employment and I have no choice but to acquiesce to her demand."

My head started to spin. "Wait, what?"

"You have many talents, Ember. I have no doubt you'll land on your feet."

I gripped the edge of my seat. "You're *firing* me?"

"I have no choice in the matter. Your aunt owns the newspaper. I am only its editor-in-chief. I tried to reason with her, of course, but she's a stubborn witch, as you know, and she would not be persuaded."

I tried to flee the table, but the vampire's reflexes were too quick for me. He grabbed my hand and urged me back to my seat. I dropped down in a daze. There was no marriage proposal and now there was no job either.

"She pointed out that it was only her good graces that afforded you the position in the first place," he continued, "and what Hyacinth giveth, Hyacinth may taketh away."

It wouldn't have surprised me to learn that steam emanated from my ears. "So not only is she forcing me out of a job I love, but she's forcing my boyfriend to be the one to lower the axe," I said in disbelief. That was a new low, even for my aunt.

"As I mentioned, she has a vindictive side. She's angry right now and wants to let you know."

"Message received loud and clear," I said. Unfortunately, it only made me more secure in my decision not to hand over Ivy's power.

"You have to understand. She's accustomed to getting her way."

"Like I said. Angry toddler syndrome." My heart pounded in my chest. "This is the behavior my father was protecting me from. This is the kind of thing she would pull with him when he didn't do what she wanted. She resented my parents for standing up to her. I bet she was happy when my mother died. One less obstacle in her way."

If my aunt couldn't control the situation, she threw a tantrum. Unfortunately, she was able to throw the kind of tantrum that forced me into the unemployment line.

"I know it seems terrible…"

"It *is* terrible," I insisted. "Couldn't you do *something*?"

He splayed his hands. "What would you have me do?"

"I don't know. Threaten to quit. She wouldn't want to lose you. She relies on you too much."

"You'd be surprised what she'd be willing to tolerate to get her way."

I curled my fingers around the stem of my glass. "No, I don't think I would be."

I stared outside at the twinkling lights below. Other than an aerial view on a broomstick, this vantage point provided the best view of the town. We'd been so happy here. I should've known it would only be a matter of time before our life here collapsed in a heap of rubble. We'd been too lucky.

"Will you hire someone to replace me?" I asked.

"I doubt it. Bentley has been eager to take on more, so this seems like the right time to appease him."

"I guess somebody should benefit from my aunt's revenge scheme."

"If you need money…" he began.

I held up a hand. "I'm not taking any of your money. Marley and I have always gotten by. This time won't be any different."

"I'm truly sorry, Ember. You have no idea how hard this is for me."

I choked back a laugh. "Hard for you? You're not the one

losing your job." I knew my decision to stand up to my aunt would have consequences, but I wasn't expecting this level of retaliation. I expected to be left off the guest list for Sunday dinners and maybe shunned at coven functions. I thought she might even try to break in and steal Ivy's belongings from the cottage, which was the reason we added the protective plants. I did not, however, anticipate this.

"You're a resourceful witch. As you said, you'll get by." Alec removed his napkin from the table and placed it on his lap.

"What are you doing?" I asked, gobsmacked.

He glanced down at his lap. "I always use a napkin, Ember. Would you expect me to dine without one?"

"Not the napkin! You just fired me, Alec. You fired your own girlfriend. Do you really expect me to sit through dinner with you like nothing happened?"

He seemed to be at a loss for words. "I don't know what you'd have me do. I thought we'd enjoy a nice meal and commiserate together. I'll pay the bill, of course."

"You can't have it both ways, Alec." I shot out of my chair, my cheeks burning. "Enjoy your nice meal. I'm leaving."

"Ember, please."

I stormed out of the restaurant before he could stop me, not caring who saw me and reported back to my aunt. I had no doubt she was thrilled to mess with my personal life as well as my professional one. The witch had no shame.

As I reached the elevator, the server appeared at my side. "I believe you left this behind, Miss Rose." She pressed the champagne bottle into my hand and I noticed she'd put in a stopper.

"Thank you."

"I think you need it more than Mr. Hale does," she whispered.

I wasn't about to argue. I hugged the bottle to my chest

and stepped inside the elevator. Once alone, I closed my eyes and willed the world to melt away.

CHAPTER FIVE

I couldn't go straight home after leaving Alec at the restaurant. I didn't want to risk Marley seeing me in my current state, although I hoped she was asleep. My hands trembled as I called Linnea and asked her to come and collect me.

My cousin didn't ask any questions. She pulled in front of the restaurant and I got into the passenger seat without a word. If I dared to speak, I knew the floodgates would come crashing open.

"We're going to Aster's," she said. "I have guests at the inn and they've all congregated on the main floor."

I cleared the emotion from my throat. "Are you sure you can get away?"

"Oh, definitely. They're entertaining themselves with an old-fashioned game of charades. It's nice, actually."

It only took five minutes to arrive at Aster and Sterling's house. I kept the car window cracked to prevent myself from hyperventilating.

Linnea parked the car in the driveway and looked at me. "Whatever it is, it's going to be okay."

I nodded, grateful my cousins hadn't abandoned me. Aunt Hyacinth could easily have tried to force their hands as well.

We entered the foyer of the beautiful house where Aster was already pacing the floor, waiting for us. Strands of her white-blond hair were falling out of its high ponytail and flecks of mascara dotted the area under her eyes.

"I come bearing gifts," I said, waving the bottle of champagne.

"Thank the gods. I could use a drink. The twins are out-of-control tonight. They refuse to go to bed," Aster said. She looked ready to dissolve into the floorboards.

"I'll get the glasses," Linnea said, bustling into the kitchen.

"Sterling, you're in charge," Aster shrieked.

"Doesn't seem like it to me," Linnea murmured.

"I'm trying," Sterling called from upstairs. He sounded ready to hurl himself over the railing.

"Why are they so energetic tonight?" I asked, leaning my elbows on the counter while Linnea rooted through the cabinet for glasses.

"They went to a birthday party," Aster said. "There was a bouncy castle and Aspen ate so many sweets that he threw up on the birthday boy. Unfortunately, the sugar's still in his system."

"I don't miss those days," Linnea said.

They both looked at me, expecting a similar remark. "Marley didn't go to many parties," I admitted. And certainly not one with a bouncy castle. When you lived in a small apartment, as many kids in our area did, you had your party at Chuck E. Cheese, if you were lucky enough to have one at all.

"What happened?" Aster asked. "Linnea said she picked you up from the Lighthouse."

"I was having dinner with Alec," I began.

At that moment, Ackley and Aspen rounded the corner

into the kitchen. They were clad in matching footie pajamas and their hair was still damp from the bath.

Aster stiffened at the sight of them. "Sterling!"

I had to admit, it was mildly amusing watching uptight Aster melt down over her children running amok.

"I'm coming." Sterling appeared in the kitchen with his shirt unbuttoned and his tie loosened. In fact, he seemed ready to hang himself with it.

"Hello, Sterling," I said. "Pleasant evening?"

"Yes, of course," he said, ever polite. "Boys, will you please do as you're told and come back upstairs?"

"We want to stay here," Ackley said and stomped his foot.

I was tempted to cast a quick spell on the twins, but thought it best not to insert myself into their domestic issue.

"I know where we can go to retain our sanity," Aster said. "Follow me." She escaped out the back door with Linnea and I right behind her. Linnea carried three glasses and I carried the bottle.

A pink and green shed took center stage under a floodlight in the backyard, alongside a bed of pink flowers. Leave it to Aster to color coordinate her shed with her garden.

"Sterling and I have been testing different sheds for the company and we decided to keep this one for me," Aster said.

Aster had recently started a business called Sidhe Shed that sold attractive 'she-sheds' for women who wanted personal space without straying too far from home for it.

"It's already proving useful," Linnea said.

We ducked into the small structure and I was amazed by how spacious the interior seemed. Pink and green bunting was strung across the back wall that spelled out Aster's name. There was a sleek silver desk and matching chair, along with a hot pink settee. Linnea and I shared the settee while Aster sat behind the desk.

"I love this," I said.

"It's my sanctuary now," Aster said. "If I'm anywhere in the house, the boys are sure to find me. They prefer my help to Sterling's no matter what they're doing."

"Typical," Linnea said. She poured the champagne into the glasses and we each took one.

"What's new with everyone?" I asked. I needed to ease into the difficult topic. If I launched right into it, I might collapse on the floor of the shed and have to be carried out.

"I have news," Aster said. "Sterling has decided to work with me in launching the business."

Linnea gasped. "Are you serious?"

Aster nodded. "It isn't official yet. He still has to give notice."

"That's huge," I said.

"We discussed it at length and agreed that it would be nice to work together," Aster explained. "It would also allow us to spend more time as a couple and home with the boys."

After seeing tonight's spectacle, I wasn't sure whether that was a blessing or a curse.

"Nothing new to report on my end," Linnea said. "The inn is busy, which is nice. Wyatt is away for a few days. A bachelor party in some resort town." She rolled her eyes.

"The sheriff has hired a new deputy," I said. "I'll be interested to hear Wyatt's reaction to her."

Linnea groaned. "I can already guess."

"When did you meet her?" Aster asked.

"I stopped by to ask the sheriff for his notes on his father's murder."

Linnea and Aster exchanged glances.

"Why would you do that?" Aster asked.

"It was Bentley's idea. He wants a big story, although I guess he'll get all the big stories now."

"What do you mean?" Aster asked.

I took a long sip of champagne. "I got fired."

The sisters wore matching shocked expressions.

"Whatever for?" Aster asked.

"For not doing what your mother wanted," I said. "She's decided to go full throttle on revenge."

Linnea rubbed my back. "I'm so sorry, Ember. Mother can be horrible."

"You've been a wonderful reporter," Aster added. "A real asset to the paper. She'll regret this."

"I haven't told you the worst part," I said. I took another long drink—liquid courage to the rescue. "She had Alec do the firing."

The sisters reeled back.

"She did what?" Linnea squawked.

"You can't be serious?" Aster said. "That's so spiteful. I can't believe…"

Linnea cut her off. "Of course you can believe it. Don't you remember that time when I was sixteen and I wanted to go to the Balefire beach party?"

"The one for Emery Stone-Bush?" Aster asked.

Linnea swallowed a mouthful of booze and nodded. "Her sweet sixteen. Everyone I knew was going, but Mother said I wasn't permitted to attend a birthday party on the beach like some commoner. It wasn't fit for a lady of my stature."

I whistled. "And I thought she took the whole Rose thing seriously now."

"Oh, she was much worse back then," Linnea said. "She's mellowed quite a bit."

I shuddered to think what non-mellow Hyacinth had been like. No wonder my father had disappeared into the night with me.

"Anyway, I did a spell to make it look like I was asleep in bed and snuck out to the party," Linnea said.

"Which obviously didn't end well for you," I said.

Linnea chewed her lip. "Mother sent Simon to find me. I saw him across the beach and knew I was deep in it."

"What happened? Did he embarrass you in front of all your friends?"

"Oh, no. That's not how Mother operates. She wouldn't have a scene." Linnea sipped her drink and licked away the bubbly residue. "She only sent him to let me know that she was aware of what I'd done. She waited until the next day to exact punishment. I spent the whole night shaking in anticipation."

"I'm afraid to ask what she did," I said. I didn't envy my cousins, growing up under Aunt Hyacinth's iron fist.

"She took away all magical privileges for a month," Linnea said.

"That's not so bad," I said. I expected much worse.

Linnea smiled. "Oh, I'm not finished."

"Mother made her do all Simon's chores for a month without magic," Aster said. "Every day after school, Linnea would have to finish her homework and then start chores. They'd take her until bedtime. Florian and I were terrified it would happen to us."

"It's no wonder I ran off with Wyatt," Linnea said. "Mother's punishment always seemed more excessive than the crime."

"That explains why you and Florian weren't the rebellious children that Linnea was," I said. "You saw the consequences of those actions."

"I never really thought about it like that, but I suppose you could be right," Aster said. "I just thought I was naturally dutiful."

"And Florian is too lazy to be rebellious," Linnea said. "Unless it involves someone of the opposite sex, of course. Then he puts in effort."

"That's unfair," Aster said. "He's been doing an amazing job on the tourism board."

"That he has," Linnea said. "I stand corrected." She sighed deeply, staring into her glass. "Sometimes I wonder what kind of man Wyatt would've become had his father lived. Maybe he wouldn't be so wild."

"Maybe you wouldn't have been so attracted to him, though," I said. "You have to admit, untamed Wyatt can be charming."

"Oh, I fully admit that. I have two children to prove it," Linnea said, smiling.

"And maybe Granger wouldn't be the upstanding citizen that he is," Aster said. "Maybe he would've been the wild, younger brother instead."

"He has said that his interest in law enforcement came about because of his father's case," I said. "Granger Nash might be someone else entirely if not for his father's death."

"Well, I like Granger as he is," Linnea said. "So I suppose that's one upside of his father's death."

"I can't imagine him any other way," I said. "Being the sheriff suits him."

"I can't believe Alec fired you," Linnea murmured. "Is that why I picked you up from the restaurant?"

I nodded. "He expected me to have dinner with him afterwards. Can you believe it?"

"Men are such fools," Aster said.

"My job isn't the only victim in all this," I said. "Marley's having trouble at school. It seems some members of the coven have become aware of my issues with Aunt Hyacinth and decided that Marley is now fair game as a target."

Aster pressed her hand flat against her chest. "Witches are bullying her because of Mother?"

"Apparently." I told them about some of the spells they'd used against Marley.

"Well, we can't let that stand," Linnea said. "Marley may be above retaliation, but I'm not."

I laughed. "Must run in the family. I've been looking up spells to see how I might help without Marley knowing."

Linnea stood abruptly and nearly bumped her head on the side of the shed. "I'll need their names."

"You're going to do something *now*?" I asked.

"Why not? This is our family's fault and so I feel obligated to offer a solution," Linnea said.

"This isn't the whole family's fault," I argued.

Linnea placed a firm hand on my shoulder. "Marley is a member of this family and Aster and I are not going to let those little punks get away with this. Are we, sister?"

Aster shifted uncomfortably. Revenge magic wasn't really her style. "Perhaps we should alert the academy…"

"Nonsense," Linnea said. "That'd be like waving a red flag in front of a minotaur." She stopped and smiled. "Rick loves that game. I wear a red lace teddy…"

Aster clamped a hand over her sister's mouth. "Thank you for sharing."

"What did you have in mind?" I asked.

Linnea's full lips curved into a mischievous smile. "Remember that spell Florian used on the wizard on the soccer team that was pestering him?"

Aster pressed her lips together. "I don't recall."

"No, you were too busy looking the other way so you didn't get caught up in any of it." Linnea rolled her eyes. "Aster's like Mother in that way."

"Take that back," Aster said, her cheeks growing flushed. I couldn't decide whether it was from the alcohol or the insult.

"I will not. You never want to get your hands dirty."

I waved a hand. "You know what? Forget it. I appreciate the offer, but if we mess with those kids, we're just as bad your mom." I was angry right now and I didn't want to take that anger out on kids. It wasn't right.

"Is there anything we can do?" Linnea asked.

"I just need time," I said. I'd have to hunt for a job and the realization was enough to make me reach for the champagne bottle and pour another drink.

"If you need anything at all, please ask," Aster said.

"The kids and I will refuse to attend Sunday dinners until mother stops her nonsense," Linnea said. "It's not like Bryn and Hudson will complain."

"Don't get on your mother's bad side on my account," I said. "She'll blame me no matter what you do."

"I'm so sorry." Linnea wrapped an arm around my shoulder and squeezed. "You don't deserve this."

I sipped my champagne. "That's life, though, isn't it? Sometimes things happen that we don't deserve—both good and bad. We just have to accept it and keep going." And right now, 'keep going' involved finishing the bottle of booze.

"I really admire you, Ember. Not many paranormals would be willing to stand up to Mother," Aster said. "You should be proud of yourself for not capitulating."

"It wasn't an easy decision, I'll admit that."

Linnea leaned her head on my shoulder. "But you made the decision and you stuck to it, even in the face of adversity."

"That I did," I said, swallowing hard.

I only hoped I didn't live to regret it.

CHAPTER SIX

At nine o'clock the next morning, a strange guttural noise jolted me upright. I'd gotten up early enough to let the dog out and kiss Marley goodbye before school and then promptly returned to bed to wallow.

I reached for the phone and saw Bentley's name on the screen. I'd completely forgotten that I'd changed his ringtone to the sound of a howler monkey. My mistake. I tapped on the screen and steeled myself for an onslaught of gloating.

"This must be a good morning for you," I said.

"I have mixed feelings."

I leaned against the headboard. "Really? I would've thought a parade would be in order. You'll finally get the juicy assignments and can stop blaming me for usurping you."

"About that…" He hesitated.

"You don't blame me for usurping you?"

"No, I totally blame you. This is about my schedule. Alec gave me new assignments and I'm afraid they're going to take up a lot of my time."

I closed my eyes as the realization settled. "In other

words, you're dropping your cold case." Roy Nash's murder would continue to go unsolved.

"I'll pick it up again if I have time, but Meadow wants me to help around the house more and obviously I want to impress Alec now that I finally have the chance..."

I blew out a breath. "It's okay, Bentley. You don't need to explain yourself. I understand."

"You do?"

"Circumstances changed and you have to adapt."

"What about Sheriff Nash? You already spoke to him, didn't you?"

"I did, but the sheriff won't think you owe him anything. I'm sure he'll just be appreciative that you took an interest in the first place."

"I guess." The elf paused. "Did Alec really fire you himself?"

I tilted my head back to stare at the ceiling. "Who else would've done it? Tanya?"

"Your aunt. She's the reason, after all. The least she could have done was lowered the boom herself."

"Yes, but it was more painful to have Alec do it. She wanted to squeeze maximum agony out of the moment."

"I always knew she was tough," Bentley said. "I didn't realize she was ruthless, too."

"You don't get to wear Aunt Hyacinth's crown without being ruthless, Bentley. I would think you've written enough articles about powerful paranormals to recognize that."

"Even so, she's family."

"My father was wary enough of her to leave town and hide me from her," I countered. "Obviously with good reason."

"I know you might not believe me, but I am sorry this happened. If there's anything I can do..."

"Thanks. There isn't, but I appreciate the gesture."

"Tanya is beside herself. She's ordering you a gift basket, but she wants Alec to leave the office first so he doesn't overhear. She doesn't want to make him feel any worse."

"Where are you calling from?" I asked. It occurred to me that Alec's vampire hearing might be monitoring this very conversation.

"I'm in the supply closet with the door closed," he admitted. "To be honest, it's pretty uncomfortable. The lower shelf is digging into my back."

"I'll put you out of your misery then. Tell Tanya to go easy on the fruit unless the strawberries are dipped in chocolate and I'll see you both soon." After all, I wasn't dead, only unemployed.

"Take care, Ember."

I set the phone on the bedside table and buried my face in my hands. Bentley felt sorry for me, which meant I was officially a loser.

PP3 scurried into the room and barked at me.

"There's a bench at the bottom of the bed," I said, pointing. "You don't need my help to get up."

The aging Yorkshire terrier barked again.

"You're so spoiled," I grumbled. I flipped back the covers and climbed out of bed to assist him. I placed him on the bed and he immediately settled on my pillow, dragging his butt across the case for good measure.

"Well, that's one way to get me out of bed," I murmured.

I forced myself to shower and prepared to face the day. Loser was a state of mind and I refused to let Aunt Hyacinth get the better of me.

I cooked eggs for breakfast and tried not to dwell on the night before, which was basically impossible. I thought Alec might call to check on me, but he was probably avoiding me. He disliked uncomfortable situations and this definitely qualified.

By the time lunchtime rolled around, I decided to text him. Maybe he was waiting to hear from me first, to make sure I wasn't too angry with him. Admittedly, I *was* angry with him. If the situation had been reversed, I wouldn't have fired him. I would've told my aunt to suck it. But Alec wasn't me and I wouldn't be in this situation now if I were more like Alec.

I wandered outside to water the plants. At least I could make myself useful around the cottage while I figured out next steps. Marley would be thrilled if I took more of an interest in the herb garden. It was her pride and joy, but I knew she wanted it to be *our* project.

As I watered the garden, I was surprised to see the sheriff's patrol car driving toward the cottage. For a fleeting moment, I worried that something horrible had happened. It was only when the sheriff emerged from the car with a sympathetic expression that I realized the something horrible had happened to me.

"Is it true?" he asked.

"News travels fast," I said. "Who told you?"

"Bolan," he said, swaggering over to the garden. "Bentley needed to confirm information with him and mentioned he'd taken over your assignments."

"You didn't need to drive out here," I said. "A phone call would've sufficed."

He leaned his hip against the fence. "Thought you might appreciate a friendly face. I also have a proposition for you."

I raised my eyebrows. "Well, that sounds interesting."

He chuckled. "Not that kind of proposition, Rose."

I set down the watering can and wiped off my hands. "What kind of proposition?"

"I'd like you to finish what Bentley started."

I tucked wayward strands of hair behind my ear. "You're offering me a job?"

"Sort of. I'd like to hire you to take over the investigation. Seems like you'll have the time to devote to it."

"Even so, do you really think I can uncover information that you couldn't?"

"You know I believe in you, Rose. Besides, I'm probably too close to the subject matter to do it justice. That's probably half the reason I haven't solved it myself. I'm too emotionally invested. An effective investigation requires distance."

My head was spinning. "And you want to pay me?"

"Of course. You'll be acting as a private investigator. Spending your own time and money. You deserve to be compensated."

"But what if I don't find more information than you did?" I asked. At what point would we pull the plug?

He gazed at me for a long moment. "You're not a quitter, Rose. If anyone can do my dad justice, you can."

My heart squeezed. "Thank you. It means a lot that you'd trust me with this, but you don't have to offer me pity money. I have savings." Although I knew I'd feel better once I had another job. The fear of losing everything loomed large in my psyche.

"It's not pity money, Rose. You're doing a job for me and I intend to compensate you accordingly. That's how these things work."

"But I'm not a real P.I. I'm a reporter, or at least I was."

"Similar skills," he said. "You're naturally curious and persistent."

I smiled. "I like that you didn't say nosy and stubborn."

"I choose my words carefully when it comes to you."

I laughed. "Why is that? Afraid I'll turn you into a toad if you insult me?"

The sheriff averted his gaze. "I know you'd never do that, Rose. You're tough, but you're not vindictive like your aunt."

He was right. Although I wasn't above petty revenge fantasies, I was certainly above chopping someone off at the knees.

"So what do you say? Are you in?"

I straightened my shoulders. "I'll do it." This way, I wouldn't feel guilty about Bentley abandoning the project and it would give me something productive to do in addition to helping Arnold Palmer. Anything to keep from throwing myself a daily pity party.

"Great," he said. "I brought the file with me, in case you said yes."

I smiled. "Feeling optimistic, were you?" That made one of us.

The sheriff glanced at the garden. "It's looking good out here. You and Marley are doing impressive work."

"Emphasis on Marley," I said. "I peer over her shoulder and make encouraging noises."

He grinned. "Teamwork makes the dream work. Isn't that what you always say?"

"I do always say that." I felt a rush of warmth. It was nice to have someone who seemed one hundred percent on my side. Everyone else had a measure of conflict, but not Granger Nash. He gave serious side-eye to anyone with power, especially my aunt. I'd always appreciated that about him, but even more so now.

He swaggered back to the car and retrieved a box from the backseat. "Here are the original files from the sheriff's office as well as my notes."

"Thanks."

He set the box on the ground between us. "It won't be the same, having Bentley trail after me during an investigation," he said.

"He's a good guy," I said. "Annoying, but good." I wagged a

finger. "But don't ever tell him I said that. I prefer our antagonistic sibling rivalry dynamic."

"Noted." He tapped the top of the fencepost. "It was good to see you, Rose. Take care of yourself."

"Thanks for stopping by." I waited until he drove away to bring the box inside and open it. There was no reason to delay. It was time to put my curiosity and persistence to good use.

Raoul arrived two hours later to find me surrounded by papers on the floor of the cottage.

What happened here? A recycling mishap?

"Sheriff Nash has hired me to investigate his father's murder."

Why would he do that? You already have a job.

"Not anymore." I filled him in on the latest development.

The raccoon gaped at me. *I can't believe she would do that. It seems like only yesterday when she helped me with my gangster problem.*

"She's angry and lashing out. This is what happens when you live your whole life with no one willing to stand up to you. You can't handle it when someone finally does."

Raoul motioned to the papers. *Are you going to clean up this mess before we go? I don't mind, but I think Marley will object.*

I squinted at him. "Go where?"

We're supposed to interview the first witch on Arnold Palmer's list.

I smacked my forehead. I'd been so distracted by my own problems that I'd completely forgotten.

I scrambled to my feet. "I'll get ready now."

And by get ready, you mean put on deodorant, right? You smell like the dump, which is a perfectly acceptable fragrance for me, but I doubt Violet Bay-Moonstone will agree.

I glared at him over my shoulder as I hurried upstairs to change and—yes—put on deodorant and a bra. I tried to feel upbeat about Arnold Palmer's prospects. Maybe Violet would be turn out to be his perfect match and they'd live happily ever after. A witch could dream.

Can I drive? Raoul asked as we walked to the car.

"Of course not," I said.

He shrugged his furry shoulders. *Thought you might be depressed enough to agree.*

"I'm not depressed." I got behind the wheel and immediately turned on Billy Joel's *Just the Way You Are*.

This song is depressing.

"No, it's not. It has an uplifting message."

Raoul changed the song to *Sabotage* by the Beastie Boys. *This is more like it.*

"Appropriate," I murmured. My aunt had sabotaged my career with a single request. I pushed away the thought and focused on the music, thumping my thumbs on the steering wheel as I drove to a small cottage deep in the woods at the very edge of Starry Hollow.

"Are you sure she lives here?" I asked.

The cottage looked abandoned. The paint on the shutters had faded to a pale green and the front door appeared rusted. The gardens were overgrown, although I could tell from the wide variety of species that it had once been a thriving English-style garden.

Looks like she needs a handyman, not a familiar, Raoul said.

"She's a witch," I whispered. "She shouldn't even need a handyman."

I don't know that Arnold Palmer would like it here. Raoul surveyed our surroundings with a wary eye.

"You're a raccoon. I would think the middle of the woods would appeal to you."

It isn't the woods. It's this place. He shuddered. *I'm getting creepy vibes. If we see empty cages inside, we're not sticking around for the snacks.*

"Opting out of snacks? Now I know you're serious." I stepped onto the 'Go Away' doormat and knocked on the door.

"You obviously can't read," a voice called. "It tells you right there how I feel about visitors."

"I can read just fine," I said. "I happen to be persistent."

"What are you selling?"

"Personalities," I said. "I have it on good authority that you're in dire need of a new one."

Raoul nudged me. *Are you out of your mind? Don't antagonize her. I don't want to end up on the menu.*

The door clicked and creaked open.

"You might want to consider WD-40 for those hinges," I said upon entering the cottage.

Violet sat in a rocking chair in the corner of the room, huddled under a fuzzy blanket. A closed book rested on her lap. I assumed she was elderly until I looked more closely and realized she was no older than me. Her auburn hair was pulled back in a severe bun and her pale skin seemed to glow in the dim light of the cottage.

"Who are you?" she asked.

"I'm Ember Rose and this is my familiar, Raoul."

Raoul saluted her.

Violet inclined her head. "You're a Rose? As in *the* Roses?"

"One True Witch, yada yada. Yep, that's me."

Violet peered at me. "I expected you to be taller and blonder. And prettier."

"Well, we're off to a grand start," I said, forcing a smile. "Why are you playing the role of a geriatric witch when you're clearly under thirty?"

Violet regarded me coolly. "There's nothing wrong with favoring a rocking chair."

"I'm not just talking about the rocking chair." I motioned toward the door. "Your garden is so overgrown, it could be hiding a family of trolls."

Raoul glanced toward the door. *The garden suddenly seems more interesting.*

Violet glowered at me. "Have you come to my cottage to insult me? Doesn't seem very wise. Impolite, too."

"Well, I agree with you on the impolite part," I said.

"And what have I done to deserve the attention of the Rose family?"

I laughed. "Oh, I'm not here on behalf of my family. I'm on the naughty list, so I'm not even allowed to attend Sunday dinners anymore."

Violet eyed me with renewed interest. "Is that so? What did you do? Use the wrong fork at dinner?"

"It's a long story."

Violet nodded at the square table with its two chairs. "Have a seat and I'll make us some tea."

I don't know that you want to drink anything here, Raoul said.

You think she'll poison us?

No, but I think she probably hasn't washed a cup in a decade.

I raised my eyebrows at him. *You bathe at the dump and you're worried about a dirty teacup?*

I expected Violet to get up to make the tea. Instead, she lifted a hand and made a zigzag motion, muttering under her breath.

"Nice work," I said.

She offered a vague smile. "I've gotten very good at doing most things from this chair."

A mug floated over to me and I plucked it from the air. *No, You Can't Have a Sip* was written in bright pink letters across the side.

"Milk and sugar?" Violet asked.

"I'm good, thanks." Normally I would've said yes, but I

couldn't imagine Violet kept fresh milk in the cottage if she couldn't be bothered to get out of her rocking chair.

"Now that I've performed the role of good hostess, what are you doing here?" Violet asked.

"We're here on behalf of our client, Mr. Arnold Palmer," I said.

"Who's Mr. Palmer?" Violet asked.

"A potential match from the agency," I said.

Violet's expression hardened. "What agency is that?"

I looked sideways at Raoul. "The matchmaking agency that sets up witches with new familiars."

"I do not need a new familiar," Violet ground out.

This was unexpected news. "You already have a familiar then?" If so, there was no sign of them.

Her lips formed a thin line. "Not anymore. Jingles died last year."

"I'm sorry to hear that."

Violet stared at the closed book on her lap. "I guess I should offer you a cookie to go with your tea. I don't know what's in the cupboard. Abby came by with groceries, but I haven't eaten much. Unless someone else cooks it, I'm not that interested."

Finally, a witch after my own heart. "Who's Abby?" I asked.

"The only friend I have left. We've known each other since elementary school. We stayed friends even after I left public school to attend the Black Cloak Academy."

"Oh, that's where my daughter goes," I said.

"Some of the witches and wizards used to make fun of me for hanging out with Abby because she's an elf, but I didn't care."

"Sounds like true friendship," I said. I sure could've used an Abby in my life when I was younger. It was a role that Karl eventually filled.

"Yeah, except when she goes behind my back and tries to get me a familiar."

"You think Abby may have submitted your name to the agency?"

Violet nodded. "Seems like something she would do, even though I told her not to get involved."

"I'm sorry. I don't want to get anyone in trouble, but it's the reason we're here."

"You work for the agency?" Violet asked.

"No, we work for Arnold Palmer, the potential familiar."

The witch glanced from me to Raoul. "I don't understand."

"Arnold Palmer is moving all the way from England for his new witch and he wants to make sure it's the right match," I explained.

Violet grunted. "Well, I am definitely not the right match, so he can leave his suitcase packed."

"Yes, I thought you might say that." I set the mug on the table. "We're sorry to have wasted your time."

"I'll have a strong word with Abby and make sure she takes my name off the list."

"I'm sure you will. Let's go, Raoul." I took the raccoon by the paw and headed for the door. "It was good to meet you, Violet. Take care now."

We left the cottage and returned to the car. Raoul looked at me from the passenger seat with disappointment in his dark eyes. *I guess we've ruled her out then.*

"Let's not be hasty," I said. I started the car and *I Dreamed A Dream* from Les Misérables blasted from the speakers.

But she doesn't want a familiar. We can't subject Arnold Palmer to someone like that after his experience with Heloise.

"Sometimes we say and do things we don't mean," I said, lowering the volume. "We took her by surprise. Maybe once the idea has time to settle, Violet will be singing a different tune."

Raoul switched off the depressing music. *Whatever it is, I hope it isn't this one.*

CHAPTER SEVEN

I DROPPED off Raoul at Balefire Beach so he could comb the sand for trash and continued into town to the Caffeinated Cauldron, where I'd arranged to meet Marianne Nash. The sheriff's mother had seemed thrilled to get my message this morning and I worried she'd be disappointed when she learned the real reason for the meeting. She was a nice woman and I didn't want to upset her by bringing up unpleasant memories.

I snagged a table in the back, away from the other customers, and mentally prepared myself for the conversation. It seemed appropriate to start my investigation with Roy's widow, even though I knew she'd encouraged her son to move on and let sleeping wolves lie.

I waved as Marianne entered the coffee shop and she threaded her way through the tables to reach me.

"I'm so glad you got in touch." Marianne sat across from me with a delighted smile. The older werewolf looked lovely in a chic blouse and skirt with a silk scarf looped around her neck.

"How are you? I haven't seen you in forever."

She set her handbag on the floor next to her chair. "I haven't had the heart to ask Granger about you. I know he acts like he's fine, but he misses you. A mother knows these things."

Warmth flooded my cheeks. I didn't want to talk about my relationship with the sheriff or anyone else. If Marianne knew that Alec and I were having issues, she might be under the misguided belief that I was here to talk about her son.

"I see him all the time, though," I said.

She gave me a pointed look. "You know what I mean."

"What can I get for you?" I asked. "I waited to order."

"A lemon-ginger tea would be wonderful."

"I'll be right back." I hurried to the counter, grateful the shop wasn't busy. I ordered the tea as well as a cinnamon latte with a shot of good fortune for me.

"I'll bring them to the table when they're ready," the barista said, once I'd paid.

"Thanks."

I returned to the table with a nervous knot in my stomach. Part of me felt cruel for raising the topic of her deceased husband. I knew she'd made peace with it, so I had to imagine she wouldn't be thrilled with this latest effort to find the killer.

"How's everything with you?" Marianne asked.

I crumpled my napkin in my fist. "Not great. I lost my job."

Marianne balked. "At the newspaper?"

"That's the one."

"But doesn't your aunt own it?" she asked, gobsmacked. "And isn't your boyfriend your boss?"

"It's complicated," I said sheepishly.

"Must be," Marianne said. "I can't imagine what prompted that."

The barista appeared by the table and set down our

drinks before rushing back to the counter to wait on a customer.

"It's not worth getting into," I said.

"I'm sorry to hear it. It's a shame Granger just hired that lovely new deputy. You'd make a fine one and we already know the two of you work well together."

"I haven't trained to be a deputy," I said. I hadn't trained for anything, really. I'd repossessed cars before I came to Starry Hollow. I wasn't exactly upwardly mobile. "Besides, Bolan would flip his Stetson if I joined the team."

Marianne blew the steam off her tea. "I think he likes you more than he's willing to admit."

"Bolan? I think you've got him mixed up with another surly leprechaun."

Marianne laughed. "What will you do now?"

"I haven't decided. I have money saved and I own the cottage outright, so luckily we're not desperate."

"I remember the panic I felt after Roy died and I knew I had to earn more if I expected to be able to take care of the boys." She shook her head. "It was a terrible period."

"I know how it feels."

"Yes, and you were even younger than I was when your husband died. What was his name again? I'm sorry to have forgotten."

"Karl."

She sipped her tea. "That's right. But you're not here to talk about our shared experiences, are you? You want to talk about Roy."

I scooped the foam off my latte with a spoon and I ate it. "How did you know?"

"Granger mentioned that someone had decided to pick up the torch. I didn't realize that someone was you."

"It wasn't initially, but now I have the time so..." I smiled. "Here I am."

"I'm glad it's you," Marianne said. "I can't say there are too many others I'd feel comfortable talking to about it."

"Then you don't mind if I ask you questions? I can understand if you'd rather not talk about it, but it would be helpful."

Marianne dropped her gaze to the table. "It was the worst time of my life. As hard as it was raising them alone, the boys are what kept me sane."

"It was the same with Marley. When you have to focus on others, it makes your own trauma easier to bear."

Marianne raised her mug to her lips. "I was able to compartmentalize, for the most part. I kept all thoughts of Roy at bay until the boys were settled in bed and then I'd let myself fall apart." She inhaled the aroma before taking a hesitant sip. "I can still remember those moments like it was yesterday."

"I would cry in the shower," I said. "It was the only place I could hide and I didn't want Marley to see me."

"I was partial to the pantry, although the way those boys ate, you'd think they lived in there." Marianne smiled. "At the end of a long day, I would pour myself a glass of whiskey, open a tin of biscuits, and wonder what really happened to my husband."

Instinctively, I reached across the table and touched her hand. I wasn't a naturally affectionate person, but I understood her pain so acutely, it was impossible not to try to comfort her.

"You're a kind soul, Ember. Sometimes it's hard to believe you're related to Hyacinth."

I withdrew my hand. "My father was determined to raise me out from under her shadow. She tried to control his life the same way she's tried to control mine."

"Sometimes the need to control comes from fear," Marianne said, "but I'm not sure Hyacinth Rose-Muldoon is afraid of anything."

I wrapped my hands around my mug. "Hers comes from greed. Nothing is ever enough for her. More money. More power. More magic. She thinks it's all rightfully hers."

She offered a wry smile. "Roy used to say she gave battle-axes a bad name."

"What can you tell me about the day he died?"

"It wasn't remarkable in any other way. School for the boys. I made a stew for dinner and made Roy promise to be home on time. He'd been working late a lot because of trouble with the business and I'd had enough of eating dinner alone with the boys." She blew the air from her nostrils. "Ironic, isn't it?"

"The file says his business was failing."

"Yes. I'd convinced him to sell, but he wasn't able to persuade Malcolm. He was supposed to have another talk with him that day, in fact."

"Do you think Malcolm had anything to do with his death?"

Marianne shook her head. "If I did, I would've looked for the evidence myself. As far as I'm concerned, the timing was a terrible coincidence."

"You don't think the argument over the business was serious enough to result in a fight? Maybe the disagreement got physical? Still could've been an accident."

"No, I don't think so. Roy was the stronger werewolf by a long shot and they both knew it. Malcolm couldn't have broken Roy's neck like that." Tears sparkled in her eyes and she dabbed at the corners with a napkin. "Sorry. It's still hard to think about the way he died. So brutal."

"I'm sorry. We can stop now."

"It's fine. If you have another question, go ahead."

"Can you think of any reason why Roy would've been found in the woods in his wolf form at that time of day?"

She shook her head again. "I couldn't think of one then and I certainly can't think of one now. He should've been on his way home from work. He wasn't like Wyatt, shifting at every opportunity. Roy was more reserved like Granger."

"Is there anyone you suspected at the time? Someone who maybe had an alibi or was ruled out for some other reason?"

Her expression clouded over. "Nothing that hasn't been covered."

"What is it?" I prompted. Something was bothering her.

"Nothing. It's hard not to think about the investigation without remembering the ridiculous rumor about Roy and Betty Hickok."

"Who's Betty?"

"A friend of ours. She was married to Barnaby."

"Was?" I queried.

"He died a few years ago," Marianne said. "Betty still lives in town, though. She sold the house and moved into a condo."

I hated to ask, but I felt compelled. "What was the rumor?"

"That she and Roy were having an affair, and Barnaby was so incensed when he found out, that he tracked Roy down and killed him."

"But you don't believe it?"

"No. I don't believe the rumor about the affair and I don't believe Barnaby killed him. They were friends. We all were. We played cards every Friday night while our boys played together."

"They have sons, too?"

"Two, just like us. They were the ideal friends, really." She sighed wistfully. "I miss those days. We'd stay up late drinking too much beer and the boys would fall asleep where they stood."

"Are you and Betty still friends?"

"Not as close as we once were. Even though the rumor wasn't true, the whole ordeal put a strain on the friendship." Marianne made a point of looking me in the eye and I knew she wanted to make it clear that, whatever the rumor had been, it was unfounded. I'd have to check the files for information on Betty and Barnaby Hickok. I hadn't made it through the whole box, so I was curious to see what else I could learn. With Barnaby dead, though, it would be impossible to bring him to justice. Either way, Granger would sleep easier knowing the truth.

"I'm glad you were willing to talk," I said. "Granger always said you wanted to leave it in the past."

"Because Granger is stubborn and determined and I didn't want him to waste his time chasing shadows. I worried it would take over his life."

"I would like to solve this for him. For you."

"If you manage it, that would be wonderful, but if you don't, that's okay too. Life goes on either way and finding his killer won't bring Roy back to us."

Despite her Zen-like words, I could see the sadness that still lingered in her brown eyes and I felt a growing sense of obligation to Marianne. I envisioned her red-rimmed eyes in the darkness of the pantry and remembered my own mottled face. I'd avoided the mirror for months back then, knowing how awful I looked.

I sucked down the last drip of latte, determined to get to the bottom of Roy Nash's death. His killer deserved to be brought to justice, but more importantly, Roy's family deserved closure.

. . .

In the evening, I ordered pizza for dinner and made sure to spend time with Marley before she went to bed. My conversation with Marianne reminded me how important it was to stay strong for the sake of my child. Although Granger and Wyatt had been teenagers when their father died, their mother still had a long road ahead of her as the sole parent and she'd done her husband proud in the end. Wyatt wasn't the ideal husband or father, of course, but he wasn't a criminal. Okay, so maybe I'd set the bar too low out of respect for Marianne.

"I should really try to learn how to cook," I said to Raoul. I sat on the sofa with my laptop in front of me, letting my mind drift.

Why? The pizza was perfect, the raccoon said. He waddled over and joined me on the sofa, prompting a momentary growl from PP3.

"I have more time to learn now and I think it would be good for me to master a new skill." Maybe I could copy a few of Marley's favorite dishes from our Sunday dinners at Thornhold.

What are you doing? Raoul asked.

"I was looking at job websites, just to see what's out there." Unfortunately, there wasn't much that interested me.

Is Marley asleep?

"Yes, for about an hour."

How did she take the news about your job?

"She's upset with Alec and Aunt Hyacinth. I told her not to worry. Jobs are a dime a dozen and I'd find another one that didn't have strings attached." The last thing I needed to do was give my anxiety-prone child another cause for concern.

Beside me, PP3 lifted his head and sniffed the air.

"Someone's at the door," I said. It was late for a visitor. As I rose from my seat, my phone pinged with a text.

Alec.

I'm outside.

My heart began to race. I hadn't heard from him, even after I'd sent him a text. My thoughts were jumbled. There was so much I wanted to say and yet part of me wanted to pretend like everything was normal.

I opened the door and my breath caught in my throat. With bloodshot eyes and paler skin than usual, the vampire looked like he'd been awake for days.

"I've come to apologize," he said.

"Come in."

Raoul's gaze darted from the vampire to me. *Should I...? Leave? That would be wise.*

I was going to say 'get popcorn,' but I guess your idea is better. The raccoon scampered down from the sofa and bolted into the kitchen.

"I'm glad you're here," I said.

Alec's face rippled with relief. "I'm so pleased to hear you say that. I thought…"

I held up a hand. "Please let me finish. I'm glad you're here because I have something to say."

Alec's shoulders tensed. "Shall I sit down?"

"No, I doubt you'll be staying long after you hear me out." A lump formed in my throat as I tried to form the right words. "A garden only thrives when it's cared for. If you plant the seeds and then ignore them, they don't grow."

"Don't be too hard on yourself. I think you and Marley have done splendidly with the garden," he said.

"I'm not talking about the garden. I'm talking about us." I was too tired to expand on the analogy. "I feel angry and disappointed in you."

"In me?" He stared at me with the kind of smoldering intensity that nearly made me lose my train of thought, but I forced myself to stay the course.

I lifted my chin. "That's right. You."

"Because I had to fire you?"

"It isn't just that, although it was the straw that broke the camel's back. I think maybe the relationship has run its course. We're making an effort more often than we're making..." I glanced away. If I looked into those mesmerizing eyes, I'd be lost. "We have incredible chemistry and enjoy each other's company, but it isn't enough, Alec. Every time I've tried to dig deeper, you've put up your wall. I don't want to have a superficial relationship with you. I want more than that, but I don't think you're willing."

"It sounds like you've been thinking about this longer than a day," he said.

"It's been on my mind, yes. I wanted to believe that love would be enough, that it conquers all, but I don't believe that anymore."

He rubbed the back of his neck. "And if I hadn't fired you, would we be having this conversation?"

"Maybe not tonight, but eventually." My voice cracked on the last word. I knew this conversation would be difficult, but I'd underestimated just how much.

The vampire stood quietly for a moment and finally nodded. "I only want what's best for you, Ember. That's all I've ever wanted."

Tears welled in my eyes and I blinked them away. "Then why not try harder?"

"I have." He cleared his throat. "Truly, I have. You must understand that I've been this vampire for a long time. It could take your entire lifetime for me to progress to the point where you want me to be."

I gulped for air. "Then you don't think I'm making a mistake?"

He cupped my cheeks in his hands. "Selfishly, I want to say yes, but it would be a lie. You deserve an amazing life and

I've come to realize I'm not the one who can give it to you. I believed I could or I never would have pursued you in the first place, but now…"

Tears splashed onto my cheeks. "Now what?"

"I know my limits. You've shown them to me, Ember, and for that I'm eternally grateful. But you deserve better than what I can offer you."

I wiped away a stray tear. "How is that I planned to break up with you, but now it feels like you're breaking up with me?"

He kissed me gently on the lips. "I'm sorry."

"Do you love me?" I asked.

"Inasmuch as I'm capable of loving anyone," he replied.

"That's a non-answer."

"It's the best one I've got." He released me and took a step backward. "I hope you'll bear me no ill will. I wish you the best of everything, as you richly deserve."

I sniffed, not wanting his last glimpse of me to include a face covered in snot. "You're better than you think you are, Alec. I wish you could see yourself the way I see you. The way Marley sees you."

He lowered his head. "By the devil, I wish that, too."

"Thank you," I whispered. I couldn't quite manage full volume.

"For what?"

"For trying. For letting me see the real Alec, even though it wasn't as deep as I wanted to go. It was a lot for you—I get that and I appreciate it."

He managed a sad smile. "You will always be the one who got away."

"If you wrote that in red comic sans font, it would be more sinister than romantic."

"You are the only one who's ever made me laugh," he said.

"I can't fully express what that's meant to me, to have light to combat the darkness."

"I'm sorry I couldn't be more."

"You were enough. Please don't think otherwise."

I blinked and heard the soft click of the door as the vampire left the cottage. I sank down, missing the sofa cushion and landing on the floor. I ignored the shooting pain that traveled up my spine, my gaze stuck on the empty doorway. It was really over.

Alec was gone.

CHAPTER EIGHT

Despite my desire to remain in the fetal position from now until the end of time, somehow I managed to drag myself out of bed the next morning. I meandered downstairs without bothering to brush my hair or my teeth. PP3 glanced at me briefly before lowering his head. Even the dog seemed to sense my need for solitude.

I entered the kitchen and stared blankly at the counter, forgetting what I wanted.

"Mom?"

I turned around to see Marley in her school uniform. "What time is it?"

"I'm about to head to school. Are you okay? You look sick."

"I'm definitely suffering from something," I said.

Marley didn't say anything. She simply crossed the room and threw her arms around me.

"Alec and I broke up," I said.

"It's going to be okay," she whispered.

"I know it will." Eventually.

She released me and took a step backward. "Maybe I should stay home from school and keep you company."

"Absolutely not," I said. "I can take care of myself. I'm going to mope around here playing maudlin music and eat ice cream for breakfast like any self-respecting woman after a breakup."

"We can watch rom-coms tonight," Marley suggested. "They always cheer you up."

"We'll see." I wasn't sure what I wanted to do in five minutes, let alone in five hours.

Marley put the kettle on. "I'll make you a drink before I go. Just sit down at the table and don't worry about anything."

I felt like I was moving in slow motion. Eventually I arrived at the table and sat. My head felt too heavy for my neck and I rested my forehead on the cool slab of wood.

"A new job is exciting," Marley said. "Try to focus on that. The world's your oyster now."

I turned my head to face her so that my check pressed against the table. "No, the world is *your* oyster. Once you get to be my age, there's no oyster. Only an empty shell."

"Wow, that's depressing." She opened a box of granola and poured some into a bowl. "I bet there are cool jobs in Starry Hollow, though. What about being a guide for the broomstick tour? You love to fly."

"I like it as a mode of transport. I'm not sure how I'd feel about it as a job," I said. It couldn't pay very much and I had college tuition to consider now that Aunt Hyacinth wouldn't be footing the bill.

"What about writing articles for another publication?" she asked. "You've really enjoyed working as a reporter."

"That would be my first choice, but there aren't many options. Newspapers are dropping like flies and it's the investigation I like more than the writing itself."

She delivered the bowl of granola to the table along with a spoon. "Can I make you coffee or tea?"

"No, thanks. You focus on getting yourself ready for school. That's the priority."

"I can help you job hunt when I get home," she said.

"Right now, I'm going to focus on Roy Nash. If a job lead comes up, then I'll pursue it, but I can't let this case fall between the cracks. It's bad enough that Bentley dropped the matter to take over my job."

She hugged me again. "Won't that be amazing if you're able to find the killer? Sheriff Nash would be so happy."

"Someone deserves to be," I mumbled. And no one deserved it more than Granger Nash. The sheriff should be up for sainthood.

"I'll come straight home after school."

I pulled myself to an upright position. "I'll be fine, I swear. Don't worry about me."

"If you say so."

"How's everything at school? Are the witches still giving you a hard time?"

Her expression clouded over. "Don't worry about me. I'll be fine."

"Marley, I'm an adult who's having a moment of crisis, but it will pass. If you need my help, I'm here."

She rubbed my back. "I know you are and I appreciate it, but I'll handle this on my own."

"Don't do anything that gets you in trouble. We won't have Aunt Hyacinth to go to bat for us."

"I can make dinner tonight, if you want," Marley offered.

"Don't be silly. It's my job to keep us fed and watered." I had to put on a brave front or Marley was going to end up mothering me instead of the other way around.

"Okay." She gave me a lingering look before vacating the kitchen.

I heard the sound of the front door open and close as she left and dropped my head back on the table. The granola was going to get soggy, but I didn't care. I had no appetite. My stomach gurgled.

Okay, maybe I had a bit of an appetite, but I wasn't in the mood to eat. The only thing I wanted to do now was crawl back into bed and stay there. I resisted the urge to succumb to self-pity, though. Marley was counting on me to be a parent. Arnold Palmer was counting on me to find his match. The sheriff was counting on me to solve his father's murder. I refused to let them down. This was his father's case. His white whale.

I dragged myself to the counter where my phone was charging and tapped the screen for my list of contacts. The best way forward was to forget my own troubles and focus on helping others.

I was determined to give the sheriff the one thing he'd always wanted—closure.

I was shocked to see Bentley hovering outside the Crooked Star, an art gallery downtown. He opened his arms to hug me, but then seemed to think better of it.

"We still don't do that, do we?" he asked.

"Not unless you want my knee somewhere uncomfortable."

"Thought as much."

"What are you doing here?" I asked. "I only told you my plans out of courtesy, not because I expected you to show up."

"I have an appointment a block over in twenty minutes," he said. "I figured I'd squeeze it in. Help you on your way."

I bristled. "What makes you think I need your help?"

He lifted a hand to touch my shoulder and quickly retracted it. "We know you and Alec broke up."

My head snapped to attention. "He told you?"

"No, but it was obvious when he called out this morning that something was wrong. Tanya spoke to him and put two and two together."

"Wow. He didn't show up for work?" That spoke volumes. Alec used work as a coping mechanism. If he couldn't manage to get to the office, the vampire was in rough shape. The thought gave me no pleasure.

"Tanya is going to check on him at home later," he said. "So don't worry about Alec. We've got eyes on him."

I was more worried about me, but I didn't need to share that with Bentley. Alec had lifetimes of experience getting by on his own and a truckload of money in the vault. The vampire would rise like a phoenix from the ashes.

"So this is where Malcolm Kincaid works now," Bentley said, glancing at the art gallery. "A far cry from co-owning a business."

"It doesn't seem like he was cut out for being his own boss," I said. "His judgment was pretty poor."

Bentley arched an eyebrow. "Poor enough to include murder?"

"I guess we'll see."

"You should let me take the lead," Bentley whispered as we headed to the door.

After last night, I didn't have the strength to argue. If the elf wanted to do some heavy lifting before he completely abandoned the case, then I was willing to let him.

The door swung open, revealing Malcolm Kincaid. The security guard stood just inside the entrance of the gallery in a white shirt and black trousers. His security badge was the only sign of his role in the gallery. His hands were clasped behind his back and his eyelids seemed heavy, as though he was either bored out of his mind or tired from an interrupted night. Life didn't appear to have been kind to him. According to his file, the werewolf was only sixty, but his thinning white hair and deep creases suggested a life hard-lived.

"Mr. Kincaid?" Bentley inquired.

The werewolf looked him up and down with suspicion. "Who wants to know?"

"My name is Bentley Smith and this is my associate, Ember Rose. We'd like to ask you a few questions."

"Can't you see I'm working?" he snarled.

I regarded the empty gallery. "Yes, but there's no one here."

"I don't guard the customers," he said. "I guard the artwork."

Bentley snorted. "You call that artwork?"

I took a closer look at the content on display. Every piece was a different artist's interpretation of the night sky.

"I actually think they're pretty," I said. Most of them, anyway. One seemed to be the artist's expression of a black hole sucking everything into its vortex—that one was the stuff of nightmares.

Bentley pressed on. "We want to talk to you about an old business partner of yours, Roy Nash."

Kincaid seemed momentarily startled. Then his wide eyes narrowed. "Why on earth would you dredge all that up now?"

"His murder's never been solved," Bentley said. "As his former friend and business partner, doesn't that bother you?"

"Of course it bothers me," Malcolm said. "Sometimes I still dream about him and, when I wake up, I think he's still alive."

"You think he's still alive?" Bentley asked.

Malcolm shook his head. "No, no. I mean, there's that

moment between being asleep and awake where I forget he's dead. That's all. Once I'm fully awake and remember..." He exhaled. "It's never easy to lose a friend, especially someone I spent as much time with as Roy."

"We understand you were the last one to see Roy alive at the office," I said.

"That's what the sheriff told me," Malcolm said.

"And is it true you had no alibi?" Bentley prodded.

"Why would I?" Malcolm asked. "Roy and I worked alone. We had no staff. Roy said he was heading home for dinner, but he never made it, so yeah. I guess I was the last one, except whoever killed him, of course."

"According to the records, you and Roy were on the outs at the time," I said.

Malcolm huffed. "Do I really need to explain myself again? I told the authorities at the time and I told young Nash the same thing when he came sniffing around."

"We'd like to hear it from you," Bentley said. "It's the reporter in us. We've read the file, of course, but much better to get it straight from the source."

The door opened and a stylish couple brushed past us to enter the gallery. They looked to be in their forties with ample discretionary income if their clothes and accessories were anything to go by.

Malcolm shuffled backward a few steps so we weren't blocking the entrance. "I don't think now is the time for this conversation," he said in a gruff voice.

I turned to see the couple migrate to the far end of the gallery. "They won't hear a thing, please."

Bentley stuffed his hands in his pockets. "You're on the clock for a few more hours, Mr. Kincaid, and we've got nothing but time."

The werewolf's shoulders sagged as he relented. "Business

wasn't going well then. Roy felt like it was a money pit and he wanted to sell and move on to something else."

"But you didn't?" I asked.

"No, I didn't. Truth be told, I was stubborn and, in hindsight, Roy was right."

"The business failed?" Bentley asked.

Malcolm laughed. "Would I be here now if it hadn't? I should've listened. Maybe if I had, he'd still be alive."

"What makes you say that?" I asked.

"Just that we'd quarreled that day and I think he probably left work earlier than he needed to," Malcolm said. "If we hadn't been arguing, maybe he wouldn't have encountered whoever killed him."

"Why did the sheriff rule you out as a suspect?" I asked.

Malcolm stood on his tiptoes and yelled, "Don't touch that, please."

I turned to see the woman snap back a hand and lower it to her side.

The werewolf shook his head ruefully. "Why do they think they can touch the artwork? Nobody needs their oily fingers on a canvas they haven't purchased."

Well, Malcolm clearly took his job very seriously.

"The sheriff ruled me out because I'm not guilty," Malcolm said.

Bentley and I exchanged looks. "That's not a reason," the elf said. "There must've been evidence that exonerated you."

"They couldn't place me at the scene and a witness said they saw me leave the office at seven, which was well after the time of death."

"You could've gone and come back without being seen," I said.

"Except his body was found in the woods near a thicket of poison oak." He paused. "I'm severely allergic. Break out in hives and everything. If I had been within a foot of that area, it would've been obvious to anyone with eyes."

I recalled Kincaid's healer's record in the file and the mention of the allergy.

"One last question, Mr. Kincaid, and then we'll leave you to get back to work," I said.

"Go on then," he urged.

"If you don't mind me asking, who do you think killed Roy Nash?"

A breath of surprise escaped him. "No one's ever asked me that," Malcolm said. "I honestly have no clue. I wish I knew, though. Roy was the best of us. He deserved better, may the gods rest his soul. His family deserved better. For someone to do that to Roy…" He closed his eyes as though willing the memory away. "They must've had a lot of anger in their heart to do a thing like that."

I was inclined to agree. Nothing had been taken from Roy, not even his wallet.

Bentley glanced at the clock on his phone. "Ooh, I need to go or I'm going to be late."

"I thought you had nothing but time," Kincaid said.

"I had twenty minutes." The elf clapped me on the back. "This one has an eternity, though. Hey, maybe you could get a job here. Is the gallery hiring?"

I elbowed Bentley in the ribs and he doubled over. "Thanks for your time, Mr. Kincaid," I said.

Kincaid chuckled. "We could certainly use someone like you in security. Plenty of customers get handsy with the artwork and sometimes even with other customers."

"I'll keep that in mind," I said, escaping the art gallery.

In the deepest, darkest recesses of my mind.

. . .

I sat on a bench near the Phoenix Club and studied the map from Roy Nash's file. According to the markings, Roy's body was found in the woods not very far from the heart of town. Investigators never figured out what prompted Roy to enter the woods instead of heading straight home from work. The theories ranged from 'wanted to relieve the stress associated with work by shifting' to 'meeting a secret lover' to 'killed elsewhere and dumped there.'

I scanned the notes for what seemed to be the fiftieth time. Accidental death had been ruled out because of the type of injury to his neck. According to the report, if Roy had simply tripped and fallen, the break would have had a different appearance.

I closed the file and rose to my feet. It was a sunny day and I needed the fresh air, so I decided to retrace Roy's steps from his former office to the spot in the woods where his body was discovered. Although I knew there'd be no physical evidence all these years later, I figured the trail might trigger a few new ideas. My father used to say he did his best thinking during a walk in the woods and how much he missed having a forest nearby in New Jersey. He'd told me that sitting against a live oak in Starry Hollow was one of his favorite pastimes.

I walked to the address of Roy's former business. The building now housed a healing supply company. I didn't bother going inside; there was nothing to learn there. I lingered in front of the entrance and tried to channel Roy. He'd left the office feeling disgruntled with his business partner and knew his wife was waiting to serve dinner until he came home. Knowing what I did about Roy's character, would he have decided to take a quick run through the woods to alleviate stress, knowing his wife and sons were waiting for him?

No. He wouldn't have.

I took a moment to survey the surrounding area. There were two neighboring buildings, both with windows and doors that faced Roy's office. The records showed they were here at the time of his death and the witness who'd seen Kincaid at seven had worked in one of them. If someone had killed Roy in the parking lot and carted his body off to the woods, chances are there would've been at least one witness to that event, yet the acting sheriff had canvassed the area with no results.

Could Roy have been meeting a lover and their tryst interrupted by the lover's jealous husband? Betty Hickok was the only potential paramour and even Marianne didn't believe the rumor. Still, it was worth a conversation with Betty. If Barnaby had been the one to murder Roy, then Betty likely knew the truth. Maybe she'd be willing to tell her side of the story after all these years—now that Barnaby was beyond the long arm of the law.

I followed the map and walked along the sidewalk to the nearest entrance to the woods. It was a well-worn path favored by hikers, although maybe it hadn't been so popular then. Along the way, I passed a couple pushing an off-road stroller, a few joggers, and two cyclists. Plenty of traffic.

The light dimmed the further I ventured, the canopy of trees blocking out the sun. It would've appeared much the same on the evening Roy walked this same path.

I glanced at the map again to remind myself where to diverge from the path. I located the narrow trail, nearly obscured by bushes, and followed it until I arrived at a small clearing lined with live oaks and the thicket of poison oak. I tucked the map into my tote bag and sighed. So this was the scene of the crime.

A breeze blew past, rustling the leaves, and I hugged myself to stave off the chill. I wasn't sure whether it was the temperature of the air or knowing that the sheriff's beloved father had died here. I wondered whether he, Marianne, or Wyatt ever visited this spot. It was likely too painful for them.

The appealing smell of live oaks invaded my nostrils and I let the scent simmer. It would've smelled just the same for Roy. In fact, it would've been stronger due to his heightened werewolf senses.

I walked along the perimeter of the clearing and considered whether there was any magic that might help me. The trees were alive at the time. Did they have memories and, if so, could I use magic to access them? It seemed unlikely or the sheriff's office would've hired a competent witch for the task years ago.

I leaned my back against one of the live oaks and slid to sit on the ground, emulating my father. I closed my eyes and allowed my mind to wander. Maybe an idea would come to me if I didn't force my thoughts in a certain direction.

Laughter impeded my progress and I opened my eyes to locate the source of the sound. Two teenaged werewolves came stumbling into the clearing. The male wore a baseball cap with the high school mascot and the female clutched a bottle of ale. They both seemed surprised to see me.

"Sorry, I didn't mean to interrupt your party," I said. I still remembered the days of sneaking off with Karl for privacy. Of course that much sought-after privacy resulted in Marley, not that I regretted my daughter for one second. She was my world and my proudest accomplishment.

"How do you know about this place?" he asked.

"I followed a trail," I said. "How about you?"

His expression was skeptical. "My older brother showed it to me last year. Werewolves have been coming here forever."

"Emphasis on *werewolves*," his companion added with a snotty tone. "It's like our own special sanctuary."

Ah, teenagers.

I pushed myself back to my feet and dusted off my bottom. "Then I guess I'll get out of your way since I'm not a werewolf."

"You're also, like, twenty years too old to be hanging out here," the girl said.

"More like ten," I shot back. Okay, maybe fifteen but who's counting?

They snickered as I vacated the clearing and I heard the girl call me a loser. Although I was tempted to do a spell that introduced them to poison ivy, I decided to retain my dignity and save any spells for solving Roy's murder.

For better or worse, I was finally growing up.

CHAPTER NINE

AFTER MY VISIT to the site of Roy's death, I called Sheriff Nash from the cottage to ask whether he knew about the clearing's popularity among werewolves.

"Yeah, I'm aware," he said. "I was too young to hang out there at the time and I wasn't interested in going afterward. In fact, I don't think any wolves went there for a couple years after my dad died."

"Did anyone think it was odd that your father would've been there?" I sat on the sofa, stroking PP3's back.

"I seriously doubt he was hanging out there at dinnertime," the sheriff said. "I thought maybe he was trying to escape from someone and that happened to be the spot where his attacker caught up to him. Dad would've been familiar with the trail from his own high school days. He might've run that way on autopilot."

"But there were no witnesses in the woods, either?"

"Afraid not."

It occurred to me that if it were strange to see a woman my age there, it had to be even stranger to see someone's father—unless he was there to drag home a wayward teenager.

"Did Wyatt ever hang out there?" I asked. It seemed like the kind of place where the sheriff's older brother would've visited frequently.

"Sometimes, but only when there were wolves there to lord over. If it was too quiet, he'd find somewhere else. You know Wyatt. Always on the lookout for a party."

Not much had changed.

"But Wyatt was home at the time of your dad's death, wasn't he?"

"He was, Rose. The whole time. Don't even entertain the thought."

"Just being thorough."

"I appreciate that."

"I'm going to see Betty Hickok tomorrow," I said. Silence greeted my announcement. "Granger?"

"Yeah, I can see why you'd feel the need to do that."

"You don't mind, do you?"

"No, it's just…It was an unpleasant theory to contemplate."

I drew my knees to my chest. "But I know you contemplated it." There was no way would he have left a stone unturned simply because it made him uncomfortable.

"I didn't find any truth to it." He paused. "But then again, maybe I was too close to the subject. This is why having you review the case is a good idea. I'm not infallible, Rose."

"It would've been a strong motive for Barnaby," I said.

"I know," he said quietly. "It's just hard to imagine. Our families were really close. I don't remember even a whiff of unpleasantness between them."

"Sometimes our parents are more adept at protecting us than we give them credit for," I said, thinking of my own father and his efforts to hide me from Aunt Hyacinth.

"Any other questions?" he prodded.

"Just one," I said. "There's a note about a missing file."

"That's right. Missing File A."

I smiled at the phone. "Very imaginative. No wonder you have a career in law enforcement."

"It was missing when I inherited the box," he said. "There's nothing in there to suggest it's anything major, though. Sometimes files get lost. It's not ideal, but it happens."

"It wouldn't happen to you. You're too organized."

"Bolan's organized. I just give that impression." He paused and I sensed he had more to say. "I don't know if it's the right time to mention it, but I want to say I'm sorry about you and Hale."

I winced. "I figured word would get around quickly. I'm already a hot topic of conversation so why not add fuel to the flames?"

"I mean it, Rose. I am sorry. I want you to be happy."

I slumped against the back of the sofa. "I know you do, thanks. I'll be fine, honestly. It's not as sudden as it might seem. There've been…issues."

"No need to explain. I'm not prying. I only wanted to offer condolences. I may not be a fan of his, but he seemed to have your best interest at heart."

"He tried," I said. "We both did." I didn't want to discuss it anymore, not with the sheriff. It wouldn't be fair to cry on his shoulder.

"If you need anything, I'm here. I'll always be here for you."

I squeezed my eyes closed to keep the tears from forming. "Thanks, Granger. I'll talk to you later."

I put the phone on the coffee table and stared blankly into space. It felt strange to talk to Sheriff Nash about my breakup. We were friends, but still.

MAGIC & MISFITS

PP3 vaulted from the sofa like he was still the spry Yorkshire terrier of his youth and I worried that his legs might crumple upon impact. To my relief, he made it to the door without incident, punctuating each step with an ear-splitting bark.

I shuffled past him and opened the door. At first glance, I thought it was Hazel, finally here to apologize for catering to my aunt's whims. Upon closer examination, I realized that an actual clown stood on the doorstep.

I slammed the door shut and locked it. "Sweet baby Pennywise! What's the point of warding the property if killer clowns make it past the border?" His bright red hair, red nose, and painted face would haunt my dreams for years to come.

The clown knocked politely on the door. "Miss Rose, it's me. Simon."

I whirled around and opened the door. "Simon? What on earth are you doing in a clown costume?"

His sinister clown eyes darted left to right. "May I please come in before someone spots me? I'm trying to remain incognito."

I grabbed him by the arm and pulled him inside. "Oh, I don't think you'll have any trouble with that."

He pulled a polka dot handkerchief from his pocket and patted his brow, accidentally wiping away some of the chalky white paint. "I don't want my mistress to know I've come to see you."

I gave him a disappointed look. "Et tu, Simon?"

"You can hardly blame me, Miss Ember."

My shoulders relaxed. "No, of course not. She's your employer and has been for a long time. I'm nobody to you."

The clown regarded me with sympathy. "Not nobody, miss. Not at all. In fact, that's why I'm here."

PP3 sniffed the clown's oversized shoes and panted happily when he recognized Simon's scent.

"I appreciate the gesture, but I know where your loyalties lie, as they should. You don't need to go out of your way for me. Marley and I will be fine." We were survivors.

Simon touched the flower on his lapel and a stream of water shot me in the face. "Oh, dear. Apologies, miss. I had no idea that would happen." He handed me his handkerchief and I wiped away the water.

"What made you decide on a clown costume?"

"My employer would never suspect me to don a suit like this," Simon said.

"Ingenuous," I agreed.

"I considered tramp clown attire but grew concerned that your aunt would call security if she believed vagrants were roaming the grounds."

I squinted at him. "What's a tramp clown?"

Simon appeared taken aback. "Miss Rose, there are several categories of clowns. If I were a tramp clown, my clothing would be far more tattered."

I scrutinized his bright, oversized outfit. It was garish but not tattered. "What kind of clown are you?"

"Whiteface," he said. "I opted for traditional. There's also auguste, rodeo, mime…"

I waved him off. "I don't need to know more, thanks." The more I absorbed, the worse my nightmares would be.

"I overheard your aunt talking to Master Florian about the demise of your relationship with Mr. Hale."

"Ah, and you came to offer your condolences? That's sweet, Simon." I reached out to pat him on the shoulder pad but then thought better of it. No contact with the clown would be best.

"I came to offer more than condolences, miss. I came to offer my assistance with cleansing the cottage."

I surveyed the state of the cottage. Okay, it was a little dusty and the cushions needed a good fluff, but it wasn't in complete disarray.

"No, I think you misunderstand. I'm talking about removing energetic debris. You might want to consider it given your current state of affairs with your aunt as well." Simon angled his head toward the door. "Those plants out front will only do so much."

"And you want to help me?" I had to admit, I was touched. Simon had no reason to offer his assistance.

"Of course, miss. You and Miss Marley are family, whether you're on speaking terms with my employer or not."

My chest tightened at his kind words. "Thank you, Simon. You have no idea how much that means to me."

"I hope you don't mind, but I brought supplies. I left them outside in case you sent me away."

Tears threatened to spill down my cheeks. "I would love your help." Maybe a good cleanse would lift my spirits. It was worth a try.

Simon retrieved his bag of supplies from outside and began unloading the contents onto the dining table.

"We'll need your magic, of course, but I've participated enough times at Thornhold to guide you through the process," he said.

"Simon, you're a real gem. I can't thank you enough." It wouldn't have occurred to me to do this, even though I'd performed a similar ritual with Linnea at Palmetto House.

"I don't want you to feel alone, miss. Nobody deserves to feel that way, least of all you and Marley." He opened a box of sparkling minerals and crystals.

"You don't think I'm wrong to withhold Ivy's magic?"

"It's not for me to have an opinion." His gaze swept the room. "Music is helpful for cleansing. Do you have a Tibetan singing bowl on hand, by any chance?"

"Do I have a...? No, I don't have a Tibetan singing bowl, Simon. I do, however, possess the magical sounds of one Mr. Bruce Springsteen."

"That will do nicely, miss." The clown's bright red mouth curved into a menacing smile and I closed my eyes.

"Great goddess, please don't smile."

He covered his mouth. "Beg your pardon, miss."

I moved my hands to my hips, switching to business mode. "How do we do this?"

If I could finish before Marley came home from school, that would be best. I didn't want to remind her that Alec was no longer part of our little family. It would only make Aunt Hyacinth's absence feel that much worse. For years, I managed to avoid dating or introducing anyone to my daughter, but my careful plans fell apart in Starry Hollow. Marley was very fond of the sheriff, but she was far more attached to Alec.

"The point of this exercise is to fill the air with so much positive energy that there's simply no room for negativity. Like this." He produced a flat red balloon from his pocket and blew into it. He tied the bottom and handed it to me. "See? I've filled it with positivity and left no space for negative energy."

I stared at the balloon with trepidation. "Please don't ever hand me a balloon again, especially when dressed like a clown."

"Forgive me." He removed the flower from his lapel and used the pin to pop the balloon.

I set my phone on the table and clicked on the Springsteen playlist. A memory filled the space in my head of Alec's Springsteen karaoke performance. I immediately changed the playlist to Taylor Swift.

"He hasn't ruined Mr. Springsteen for you, has he?" Simon asked. "That would be a pity."

"It's only temporary." I hoped.

Simon began to burn charcoal discs.

"Should I turn off the smoke detectors?" I asked.

"Oh, yes. I can do that for you, miss." The task didn't take him long in the small cottage.

"Which herbs did you use in the bundle?" I asked.

"The ones for cleansing and protection. There's sage, naturally, as well as mullein leaves and damiana."

I turned to peer at him. "Damiana? Isn't that for attracting love?" I seemed to recall Artemis mentioning it on a previous occasion.

"It isn't only for that. It also promotes relaxation and the healing of relationships."

I folded my arms and smiled. "You sly clown. You're trying to slip in an herb to help my rift with Aunt Hyacinth."

Simon looked properly chagrined. "Guilty as charged, miss. You can't blame me for wanting harmony between you."

"No, of course not. Besides, healing relationships is still positive energy which is what we need in this cottage right now."

"Quite so."

Smoke billowed from the fireproof bowl and I inhaled the pleasant aroma.

"Now is a good time to focus on your intention, miss," Simon said. "How would you like Rose Cottage to feel now that your relationship has ended?"

I concentrated on my hopes and dreams for the future. It was a little challenging given my current view of a creepy clown surrounded by smoke, but I persevered. I pictured Marley laughing. Bonkers on the scratching post. Raoul with a box of pizza on the coffee table. It didn't escape my notice that I failed to place myself in the picture. Although I knew I deserved happiness, too, it sure didn't feel like it at the moment.

Simon stopped waving smoke around the room and looked at me. "Is something wrong, Miss Ember?"

"No. Yes. Well, I mean you wouldn't be here otherwise, would you?"

He mustered a smile. "I'm sorry. I only meant that you seem down and this is supposed to be an uplifting ritual. Perhaps I should have waited."

I shook my head. "You were right to come and I'm grateful for it. I'm grateful for all the good in my life, truly."

"But?" he prompted.

I cleared my throat and grabbed a bundle of herbs. "But nothing. This is about clearing the air and that's exactly what I intend to do. Just because a decision is hard doesn't make it wrong."

"No, sadly not. Indeed, sometimes the hardest decisions of all are the ones most necessary."

The cottage filled with smoke and I peered into the haze for a glimpse of my future. I poured as much positive energy as I could muster into my movements and began to feel a spring in my step as I continued around the cottage. I made my way upstairs and banished negativity from each room, including the bathroom. I spent a few extra minutes on the bed and the bedroom window, where Alec had materialized one night to confess his feelings for me.

I returned downstairs to find Simon on the sofa cushion, making sure the smoke reached the ceiling. He was thorough, I'd give him that. As the clown generated more smoke, I danced along the perimeter of the room to *Shake It Off*, shaking my bundle of herbs in time to the beat. I was so engrossed in the activity that I failed to notice PP3 barking at the door.

The front door swung open and I glimpsed Raoul and

Arnold Palmer. The raccoon screeched at the sight of the clown and yanked the door closed.

Ember, are you okay? Are you being held hostage?

"I'm fine," I called. I danced over to the door and opened it. Raoul and Arnold Palmer stood huddled together on the doorstep, trembling. "It's Simon. He's in disguise so Aunt Hyacinth doesn't recognize him."

Couldn't he have dressed as a giant squirrel or something?

"And risk looking like a furry? I don't see how that's better."

Raoul and the pink fairy armadillo moved past me to enter the cottage. The raccoon coughed and tried to dispel the smoke.

Maybe we should come back later, he said.

"We're almost finished," I said. "Did you need something from me?"

No, I have something for you. An address for Laurel Honeywell.

"How did you manage that?" I asked, tossing the bundle onto the table and dusting off my hands.

Garbage isn't only good for a snack, he said.

I cringed at the thought of my familiar dumpster diving for both snacks and information. "You know I could've just asked the sheriff for it, right?"

The raccoon smiled. *Where's the fun in that?*

CHAPTER TEN

Raoul and I left Arnold Palmer at Rose Cottage to wait for Marley to come home from school. PP3 didn't seem thrilled to share his space with the pink fairy armadillo, but I slipped the dog a chew toy as a bribe.

Arnold Palmer promised to make himself useful in the kitchen while we were gone, which was music to my ears. Someone should be cooking in the kitchen, even if it wasn't me.

Raoul and I drove to the address on Larkspur Lane. Number thirty was a small, nondescript building with a sign that read *Wonder Wings* in fancy purple letters.

"Wonder Wings," I muttered. "Sounds like she sells maxi pads."

I pushed open the door and blinked rapidly to adjust to the light. The whole room seemed to sparkle with tiny gemstones and glitter. It seemed more like a fairy enclave than the workspace of a witch.

If you're right, then these are the most exciting sanitary products on the market, Raoul said.

A petite blonde emerged from a side door and smiled

when she spotted us. She was dressed in a black jumpsuit that appeared to be entirely of beads.

"Hi, I didn't realize I had visitors," she said.

"We're looking for Laurel Honeywell," I said.

"That's me. Are you here with my dry cleaning? The owner said I'd have it by ten and it's half past." She wagged a finger at me like I was a naughty puppy. "I'm not fond of broken promises."

"I don't work for a dry cleaner," I said. "My name is Ember Rose and I've been hired by your potential familiar to see whether you'd be a good match for each other."

Laurel's smile widened. "What a terrific idea. I thought that was the whole point of the service, though."

"My client is in search of a lifelong commitment and wants to be certain the choice is right for both parties."

"I wholeheartedly agree," Laurel said. "I like this potential match already."

"What is it that you do?" I asked.

"I design embellishments for fairy and pixie wings," she said. "I started my company two years ago and it took off." She reached into a box and pulled out a single white wing lined with red gemstones.

"Wow, that's impressive. You should talk to Bentley Smith about writing an article about you for *Vox Populi*. They're always on the hunt for special interest pieces and I happen to know the editor has a soft spot for entrepreneurial women."

"I would love the chance to share my story. I want all the little witches in Starry Hollow to know they can be whatever they want to be. Follow their dreams."

Raoul rolled his dark eyes. *Yes, because little witches are regular readers of the weekly newspaper.*

"So you started Wonder Wings from the ground up, I guess," I said.

"Oh, yes." Her eyes grew round and solemn. "I only had a

fifty-thousand-coin loan from my dad to get started. I had to forgo sushi and caviar for weeks to stretch the budget."

I nearly choked on my own saliva. "Yes, I can imagine."

You're one to talk, Miss Rose, Raoul said.

Laurel craned her neck to look past me. "Where is my match? You did say it's a he, yes?" She flipped her blond hair off her shoulder. "I find females try to compete with me, so I'm much better suited to having a male as a familiar. That way there's no jealousy."

I exchanged looks with Raoul. "You're worried about your familiar competing with you?"

For what? Cans of tuna?

Laurel walked over to her desk and sat. "You wouldn't understand. When you're this attractive, everyone feels the need to compete with you. It's subconscious. I don't blame them, really, but I would prefer a familiar that knows his place and I think that works best with a male to fawn over me."

"What happened to your original familiar?"

"I never had one," Laurel said. "My parents tried to match me when I was younger, but they never found one up to snuff. I let it go for years, but I've seen so many other witches out and about with theirs." She turned one of her diamond earrings in a nervous gesture. "FOMO got the better of me, I suppose, and I finally submitted an application with the agency."

"Arnold Palmer would be a fantastic familiar for any witch," I said. "He's thoughtful, compassionate..."

"How are his paws?" she interrupted.

"His paws?" I echoed.

"I know he doesn't have opposable thumbs, but can he manipulate objects? I'd love someone who can hold my mirror in a pinch." She started ticking off ideas on her fingers. "Help me apply makeup. Hold my wand." She snapped her fingers. "And if he can wield a knife, even better. I like my onions finely chopped and I'd love to pass that task to my familiar."

I was beginning to get a bad feeling about Laurel Honeywell.

"Well, he doesn't have paws."

Her brow lifted. "Oh, dear. He's disabled?"

"No, he's perfectly able. He's a pink fairy armadillo and I think you'll find…"

She silenced me with a look. "I'm sorry. He's a what?"

"A pink fairy armadillo. A little on the pudgy side so he has trouble with lift-off, but I'm sure with diet and exercise, he'll be fully airborne again in no time."

Laurel stared at me. "Do I look like the sort of witch who would have a pudgy armadillo as her familiar?"

"I don't know. Is there a particular paranormal best suited to an armadillo?"

She jerked up her chin in a haughty manner. "I am a witch, Miss Rose. Only a cat will do."

"And I suppose you like your cats the way you like your coffee."

She frowned. "I like to give them cream?"

I bit back a smile. "Black, Laurel. You prefer a black cat as your familiar."

"Quite right. No self-respecting witch would be caught dead with anything else."

I folded my arms. "Is that so?"

Raoul tugged on my elbow. *Come on. We don't need to prove anything to her.*

I shook off his paw. "What makes you think there's only one appropriate kind of familiar for a witch? Did you learn that at the Snobby Witch Academy?"

Laurel sniffed. "I can understand why your aunt disowned you." She gave me a haughty look. "Yes, that's right.

I know who you are now. And a raccoon? I mean, seriously. What ever happened to standards?"

I was so glad we'd come to vet Laurel before Arnold Palmer met her. It would've been a humiliating meeting for the poor little guy. I couldn't believe the agency had selected Laurel as an option. Her attitude toward other species was frightful.

"Let's go, Raoul. I think we've heard enough from Miss Honeywell."

Hineysmell more like, Raoul grumbled.

"I'll find my own familiar, thank you very much. One worthy of me and I can assure you it won't be a pink fairy armadillo too overweight to get off the ground."

Raoul turned back toward the witch and began foaming at the mouth and growling.

Laurel shrieked. "He's rabid. I knew it!" She glowered at me. "No wonder your aunt doesn't want a relationship with you. You're absolute trash."

Finally, a compliment, Raoul said.

Laurel took out a wand as though she intended to cast a spell on the raccoon. Raoul lunged at her, prompting her to spin on her heel and run. He waited until she'd locked herself in the side room before collapsing on the ground in a fit of laughter.

"I'm not even going to reprimand you for that. She deserved it."

This is exactly why Arnold hired you, Raoul said. *To protect him from this kind of response.*

"I worry about the familiar she ends up with. It won't be easy for them."

Ha! No worries there. She'll never end up with a familiar for the same reason she'll never have a serious relationship. She thinks too highly of herself.

He made a good point. Laurel was destined to spend the

rest of her life alone with that attitude. Like Alec, she'd built a wall around herself, only her wall was built by insecurity disguised as ego. I wanted to feel sorry for her, but I didn't. She'd either evolve and open herself up to new possibilities or she wouldn't. The choice was hers.

What now? Raoul asked, as we left Wonder Wings.

I glanced over my shoulder at the door. "Well, I think we should rule out Laurel as a candidate."

Thank you, Captain Obvious.

"And I think we should talk to the third candidate."

Now?

"I can't now. I'm going to see Betty Hickok before it gets too late." But the sooner we could find a match for Arnold Palmer, the happier I'd be.

What if Lavender doesn't check out either? Then we're back to square one.

"Not necessarily."

You can't still be considering Violet.

"Why not?"

Because she looked like she was preparing for her villain origin story.

I cast him a sidelong glance. "We're going to have to limit your access to superhero movies."

Only if you agree to limit your access to depressing music.

I exhaled. "I'll take it under advisement."

Betty Hickok's condo building was located downtown, not far from the colorful row of houses known as the Painted Pixies. There was a large lobby with two elevator banks and I was surprised by the lack of security in a building of this size. I waltzed straight in and rode the elevator to the seventh floor. The door to Betty's condo was wide open and all I could see were cardboard boxes.

"Don't lift two at once," a throaty voice said. She sounded like Lauren Bacall after one too many cigarettes. "That one has my thimble collection."

I poked my head through the doorway. "Hello?"

A slender woman emerged from behind a tower of boxes. She wore a Starry Hollow T-shirt with sweatpants and a green bandana over her head. Strawberry blond curls peeked out from behind the fabric.

"Can I help you?" she asked.

"Hi, I'm looking for Betty Hickok."

"Are you from the moving company? No one is supposed to be here for an inventory check until tomorrow."

"I'm not from the moving company. My name is Ember Rose. May I come in?"

"Rose?" she repeated. "As in Rose-Muldoon?"

"Just Rose," I said.

"Can I ask what this is about?" She seemed more distracted than unfriendly.

"It'll take more than a minute, I'm afraid," I said. "I'm sorry to barge in. There was no security downstairs so I came right up."

"No worries. The landlord warded the whole complex to prevent any supernatural shenanigans and seems to think that takes care of security." She rolled her eyes.

"Shenanigans?" I queried.

"Magic is prohibited inside the building. I can't even shift in my own living room. It won't work. I have to wait until I'm outside."

"Who is it, Mom?" A muscular man appeared, holding two large boxes. He was well over six feet tall with brown eyes and a mess of sandy-colored hair. He grinned when he saw me. "Whatever it is, the answer is yes."

His mother swatted his arm. "Mind yourself. She's a Rose," Betty whispered. "This is my younger son, Beau."

Beau set down the boxes next to the others and shook my hand.

"I'm sorry to interrupt. I can come back if you're too busy to talk," I said.

Betty regarded the boxes with a tired expression. "It's time for a break anyway. Come in. I'll pour us a glass of lime fizz."

"Where are you moving to?" I asked, crossing the threshold.

"Arizona," Betty said. "My sister lives out there and we've decided to buy a house together. We're both getting older and think it will be nice to keep each other company now that our husbands have passed."

"She's leaving her boys behind," Beau said.

Betty reached up to ruffle his hair. "You're grown men. You don't need your mother anymore."

"Don't tell me that," I said. "I want to believe my daughter will always need me."

Betty seemed to soften toward me at the mention of a daughter. "Oh, how lucky. I wanted girls. Seems the universe had other plans."

Beau grimaced. "Here we go."

Betty opened the fridge and retrieved a glass pitcher. "I had pink clothes picked out when I had Jayce. That's my older son." She smiled at Beau. "Even kept them for this one, living in hope."

"Sorry to disappoint you," Beau said. "Again."

Betty poured three glasses of lime fizz and distributed them. "How old is your daughter?" she asked.

"The age where she's too young to drive but too old to think I know best," I said.

Betty smiled as she brought the glass to her mouth for a generous sip. "Ah, yes. I remember it well."

"What do you mean?" Beau asked good-naturedly. "We were perfect angels."

"More like perfect devils," Betty said. "Between you and your brother and the Nash boys, there was never a dull moment."

At the mention of the Nash boys, I seized my opening. "I understand you were close with the Nash family."

"Once upon a time," Betty said. Her smile turned sad. "Before Roy died."

"As it happens, that's the reason I'm here," I said. I gauged her face for a reaction.

"To talk about Roy Nash?" Betty asked. Slowly, she lowered her glass. "I knew your name sounded familiar. You write for the newspaper."

I didn't bother to correct her. "A colleague of mine cracked open a few cold case files and Roy's happened to be the one on top."

"I guess that doesn't surprise me, with Granger being sheriff," Betty said. "He's always wanted his daddy's murder solved."

"Who wouldn't?" Beau said.

"I would think you'd want that, too, being close to the family and all," I said.

Betty flinched. "Of course we do. His death was a real tragedy. Our family hit a terrible rough patch after he died."

My gaze flicked to Beau, who wore the same sad expression as his mother.

"I understand there were certain unfounded allegations made against you and your husband at the time," I said, treading carefully. I wasn't sure whether raising the subject in front of Beau was a good idea, but if Betty was in the process of moving, my opportunity for questions was limited.

Betty pressed her lips together. "Like I said, it was a challenging time."

"If it's any consolation, Marianne Nash never believed a word of it."

Betty's sharp intake of breath was audible. "How is she? I haven't spoken to her in such a long time."

"She's doing well," I said. "Settled."

"Good for her." Betty gulped down the rest of her lime fizz. "I hope to get settled again, once I'm in Arizona. It's been too hard staying here now that Barnaby's gone. We'd built our lives here."

"If you don't need me, I'm going to keep moving boxes," Beau said.

Betty smiled at her son. "I know why you're in a hurry. You have that date tonight, don't you?"

"It's nothing serious," Beau said quickly.

"No, it never is." Betty shook her head. "Maybe if I had grandbabies to look after, I'd be more inclined to stay."

Beau groaned as he left the kitchen.

"He and Jayce seem steadfast in their refusal to settle down," Betty said. "I know Marianne has the same issue, although at least she has those two grandkids." She gave me a curious look. "They must be relations of yours."

"Cousins," I said.

She leaned against the counter. "There was no affair, in case you were wondering. It was all a misunderstanding. Roy had bought a necklace for Marianne for their anniversary that year and Barnaby found it." She sighed. "Foolish man thought it was a gift from Roy."

"And that's how the rumor started?"

Betty nodded. "But Barnaby didn't kill Roy. Never even confronted him. It didn't get that far. I was able to explain the situation before Barnaby did anything stupid."

"And he believed you?" I asked.

"Of course. And Marianne got the necklace on her anniversary, as planned." She frowned. "I'm not even sure she ever knew the specifics about the misunderstanding."

"And this happened not long before Roy's murder?"

"A few weeks before, I think. It was so long ago, it's hard to remember exactly." She stared ahead, unfocused. "Some memories I'll be happy to leave behind."

"Do you have any theories as to what happened to Roy?" I asked.

"Don't I wish? I want more than anything to know the truth. To make the killer pay for what they did to Roy. He was such a good man." She fished a tissue from her pocket and blew her nose. "At least he and Barnaby are together now. I hope they're drinking beer and watching over us."

"That's a lovely thought," I said.

"Maybe I'll give Marianne a call before I go. It might be nice to see her one last time."

"I'm sure she would be happy to hear from you."

Betty nodded. "At the time it seemed like we only lost Roy, but the truth is we ended up losing the whole family."

My thoughts turned to Aunt Hyacinth and I wondered whether I'd have a similar experience. I hoped not. My cousins were an important part of my life. It would be tragic to lose them now that I'd found them.

"Good luck, Ember. I hope you find what you're looking for."

I shook her hand before I left. "Same to you."

CHAPTER ELEVEN

THE NEXT MORNING quelled my fears when Linnea showed up on my doorstep. Unlike Simon, my cousin didn't see the need to come in disguise. If her mother complained about her treachery, Linnea simply intended to ignore her.

"What are you doing?" Linnea asked.

I returned to the dining table where my laptop was open. "Researching a job. There's an opening at the Pot of Gold for a manager and I have an interview in an hour."

Linnea scoffed. "You're a Rose, Ember. You can't work at a comedy club."

I smiled at her. "And you run an inn. I thought Roses didn't do that, either."

Her expression softened. "Touché."

"The problem is I'm not qualified for anything. Your aunt got me the job at the paper."

She slid into the chair across from me. "And you've done well with that. Can't you write for another paper?"

"There are no other papers. It's a dying business as it is." As much as I enjoyed it, I didn't see an option to continue working in the same capacity.

"What about Aster's new company? She said she'd love to work with you."

"She's got Sterling now. She can't afford to pay me, too, and I need a job that's going to bring in money. I have savings, but I'd hate to burn through it all while we wait for Sidhe Shed to turn a profit."

"I'm sure one of us can loan you money…"

My head snapped up. "No, absolutely not. We're fine. I'm working on a couple of side jobs now, which reminds me—do you know Violet Bay-Moonstone?"

Linnea appeared thoughtful. "Yes, I know who Violet is. She used to volunteer for all the coven gardening events." She paused. "Now that you mention it, I haven't seen her in a long time."

"That's because she refuses to leave her rocking chair."

"I remember her familiar died. The coven held a small ceremony." She scrunched her face, appearing to think. "I wish I'd paid more attention. I was probably too caught up in my own drama to realize Violet was suffering."

"Speaking of drama, what do you know about the Hickoks?" I asked. "Did Wyatt ever talk to you about them?"

Linnea adjusted her messy bun. "Oh, yes. He had quite the rivalry with the Hickok brothers. They fought over sports, girls—you name it."

The news didn't surprise me. All that testosterone in one room had to create macho drama on occasion.

"I met Beau. He seems really nice." The werewolf was helping his mother move boxes, which was basically the definition of nice. Nobody liked being involved in a move, even when they were the ones moving.

"Beau came to our wedding. The whole family did. We didn't see much of them, though. They'd already drifted apart by then, but it seemed wrong not to invite them."

"Did Wyatt ever make any comments about the Hickoks in connection with his dad's murder?"

Linnea shook her head. "No, never. You know Wyatt, though. He's not the most communicative paranormal. That was part of the reason the marriage didn't work out."

"Yeah, about that…" I told her about Alec.

"Oh, Ember." She covered her face. "What a horrible week this has been. I'm so sorry."

"Don't worry about me. I'll be fine."

She clenched her hands into fists. "Oh, I am so furious with Mother over this."

"I can't blame her. I think he and I were headed in this direction already. Firing me just hastened things along."

Linnea started to cry. "I'm sorry. I don't mean to get so emotional. It just breaks my heart to see a relationship end."

"You're a good witch, Linnea." With a much kinder heart than her mother possessed.

She reached across the table and squeezed my hand. "Aster, Florian, and I are here for you, Ember. Whatever you need. Please don't think for one second that Mother will influence us."

"Thank you." It was nice to hear, even if I didn't entirely believe it. "The Council of Elders meeting is tonight, isn't it?"

"Why do you ask? Great Goddess. You're not going to storm the meeting and confront Mother, are you?"

"No, nothing like that. I need to speak to Arthur Rutledge. He was listed as a suspect in Roy Nash's murder and I wanted to catch him off-guard to ask him about it."

"Really? I don't remember that at all," Linnea said.

"He had an alibi, but I'd still like to talk to him. Leave no stone unturned."

Linnea smiled. "And that's one of the reasons you made such a good reporter. Mark my words. Mother will regret letting you go. In fact, I bet she already does."

Somehow I doubted it.

The comedy club was mostly empty at this hour, which was probably the reason they'd chosen this time for the interview. I'd been here a few times before, usually as part of an investigation. I certainly never expected to be here interviewing for a job.

A leprechaun scurried to the lobby to greet me. "You must be Ms. Rose. I'm Mr. Collins, the day manager."

"Ember. Nice to meet you." I shook his tiny hand.

"Why don't you step into my office? It's right this way." His small feet moved so quickly, they seemed to blur. I hurried to keep pace with him.

His office was a mess, with papers everywhere. He swept a cat off the top of the desk and motioned to the empty chair.

"Have a seat."

"Thanks for inviting me for an interview."

"Of course. Mervin says he knows you so it was a no-brainer."

"Yes, he sits on the Council of Elders with my aunt."

Mr. Collins frowned. "Oh, right. You're one of *them*."

"I wasn't raised here, though. No silver spoons in this mouth." I opened wide as a demonstration.

Mr. Collins reviewed my resume. "It says here you repossessed cars in the human world. What was that like?"

"Sad, mostly. Occasionally gratifying." Especially when there was a pompous middle-aged man and a luxury car involved.

"Do you have any experience managing staff?"

"I have a daughter and a familiar."

"I see," he murmured. He studied my resume for a long moment before looking up at me. "You're a bit tall."

"Because I'm not a leprechaun."

"And your hair is a bit dark for my taste."

"Again, not a leprechaun."

"Let's see how you look in a hat." He emerged from behind the desk and tried to place a green top hat on my head, but he couldn't quite reach. He jumped, only making it as high as my neck.

I swiped the hat from his hand and set it on my head. "Happy now?"

He inclined his head, scrutinizing me. "I don't think I am."

"Mr. Collins, why does it matter how I look? You can't reject me on the basis of physical appearance. That's discrimination."

Mr. Collins stared at me intently. "How would you feel about dying your hair and wearing green-tinted moisturizer?"

I heaved a sigh and removed the hat from my head. "I don't think is going to work out, Mr. Collins."

"But it isn't all bad. You'll be able to reach the top shelf in the break room. Nobody will be able to steal your mug."

I handed the hat back to him. "Thank you for your time, Mr. Collins, but I don't think I'm the droid you're looking for."

"It was nice meeting you. If you're in need of a laugh, come see us tomorrow night. We've got a hilarious show planned."

I rose to my feet, towering over the leprechaun. "I don't need a show when my whole life is a joke, but thank you all the same."

On the way back to my car, I noticed a Help Wanted sign in the window of Charmed, I'm Sure. Although I didn't really want to work in a potions shop, beggars couldn't be choosers. It was at least worth a conversation.

I wandered into the shop and tried my best to put on a professional face. The witch behind the counter didn't look a day over twelve. Great. Not at all awkward.

"Hi, I'm Bianca," the adolescent-looking witch chirped. "What can I help you find today?"

"A job," I said. I gestured to the sign on the window. "It says you're hiring."

The witch's mouth formed a tiny 'o.' "Right. We need a potion master. Can you do that?"

"What kind of potions?" I didn't know why I bothered to ask since I wasn't skilled enough to make potions for sale. I could barely make ones that satisfied my tutors.

"I'd have to ask my mom," Bianca said.

Her mom. Wow. Maybe she really was twelve.

"Would you like to schedule an interview?" Bianca asked.

"No, that's okay. I doubt I'm qualified." I swiveled to look at the array of potions. "Have anything for losers?"

She pointed to the left. "We have a good fortune section if you want to check it out."

I heaved a deep sigh. "I think it's a necessity at this point."

"Let me know if you need any help."

Boy, did I ever.

I meandered over to the good fortune section and scanned the options. I ignored any potions related to luck. My current situation was down to my own choices, not luck. I needed…something else.

"Ember?"

My head shot up and I looked directly into the eyes of a crazed clown, except this one wasn't Simon. "Hazel," I said.

She pressed her bright red lips together. "I didn't expect to find you in here."

"Why? Because it's magic-related? I'm still a witch whether I have my aunt's blessing or not."

"That's not what I meant," she said. Her gaze swept the

interior of the shop, probably to make sure no friends of Aunt Hyacinth were within earshot.

"I'm sorry about everything," she said.

The Mistress of Runecraft was sorry? Color me shocked. "I would think you'd be thrilled not to tutor me anymore."

"I'm sure you would think that." She fiddled with a ruby red bottle on the shelf in front of her. "Truth is that I miss our lessons. They were…fun."

I balked. "You think our time together was fun?"

"Didn't you?"

I stared at her for a long moment. "I guess maybe I did." And I learned a lot from her, too, not that I wanted to admit it.

"Your aunt has forbidden us from contacting you," Hazel said. "Otherwise, I would have, if only to explain myself."

"There's no need to explain. My aunt drives a hard bargain. I know."

Hazel hesitated. "I heard you and Alec broke up. Is that true?"

I nodded. "It's for the best."

"I can't believe she made him fire you. I would've dumped him *and* hexed him in the process."

"It wasn't an ideal situation, but I'll bounce back."

Hazel's gaze darted to the witch behind the counter and back to me. "I'm sure the whole thing will blow over with your aunt. If it's any consolation, she's been in a terrible mood."

"What else is new?"

"No, I mean it. She's been biting heads off left and right. We're all avoiding her as best we can."

"She's just angry because she didn't get what she wanted."

"Don't be too sure. I think she misses you and Marley."

Was I supposed to feel sorry for her?

"She'll have plenty of time to ruminate over her choices

while we're not speaking. In the meantime, I need a job. Do you know of anything?"

Hazel grunted. "What do you need a job for? You've got the cottage free and clear. And you must have money saved from *Vox Populi*."

"I do," I said, "but it won't last forever. I'd rather stay ahead of the bills than fall behind them." I knew how that felt and I'd sworn to myself that I'd never put myself in that situation again.

Hazel chewed her lip. "I might know of an opportunity at the Shooting Star."

"The place where they host country line dancing?"

"That's the one."

"I'd rather move back to New Jersey." Okay, it seemed I still had some standards. Maybe if I didn't have any savings, my attitude would be different.

"I can't think of anything else off the top of my head," Hazel said, "but if I do, I'll let you know."

"How? Aren't you worried my aunt will intercept your transmissions and punish you?"

"I'll send a messenger," she said. "Maybe a squirrel or something."

"Please don't. PP3 might intercept that one and it won't end well for the messenger."

The door to the shop opened and Hazel fell silent as a wizard came down the aisle.

"Good afternoon, Howard," Hazel said.

The wizard nodded in greeting and continued walking to the back of the shop.

"I bet I know where he's headed," Hazel whispered. "His wife told Marigold that Howard has performance issues."

"That seems harsh. I wouldn't want my wife sharing my bedroom inadequacies with the entire coven."

She swatted my arm. "Not like that. Get your mind out of the gutter, Rose. I meant with magic."

Oh, that made more sense.

"I should buy my potion and go before someone squeals on me," Hazel continued. "I'm glad I ran into you, though." She paused. "Have you been practicing on your own?"

"Practicing what?"

"Runecraft," she said.

I waved a hand. "Oh, no. I hate scribbling all those symbols."

She blew a raspberry. "Would it have killed you to tell a white lie?"

"Your butt doesn't look remotely big in those pants. Not even a little bit." I flashed a cheeky smile. "Is that better?"

Hazel glared at me before stomping down the aisle and I bit the inside of my cheek to keep from laughing.

By the gods, I really did miss her.

CHAPTER TWELVE

"Your slippers are by the bedroom door, miss, and I took the liberty of cleaning up the kitchen. I hope you don't mind. I can't abide a mess."

Arnold Palmer lumbered into the living area from the kitchen. Earlier he'd shown me the proper knife to use for chopping onions and together we made spaghetti Bolognese. Apparently I'd been using a steak knife to cut onions, which was half the reason I was so bad at it. The more time I spent with the pink fairy armadillo, the less I wanted him to find a witch of his own.

"Thank you, Arnold Palmer, but you didn't have to do that."

"I can tell you have a lot on your plate, miss. I'd like to do my part to help, given that you've gone out of your way to help me."

"I appreciate that." I paused. "There's only one problem."

The pink fairy armadillo looked at me with trepidation. "There's a problem, miss?"

"I don't own a pair of slippers."

"Ah, yes. I noted your size on a pair of shoes in the closet and purchased you a pair in town. With these drafty floorboards, it's advisable to have a covering for your feet."

Raoul rolled his beady eyes. *Kiss-ass.*

"You're very kind," I said. "It's a shame Heloise wasn't able to appreciate that."

"I'd like to say she was a troubled witch, miss, but the truth is she didn't possess a nice bone in her body. Heloise was selfish and disagreeable through and through."

My thoughts turned to Aunt Hyacinth. "Yes, I know the type."

I think he's punching above his weight, Raoul said.

I smiled at my familiar. *Aw, are you worried he's going to steal me away from you?*

Of course not. I know my worth.

Arnold Palmer fluttered across the room and I realized he was at least a foot off the floor.

"Arnold, have you lost weight?"

"I have, miss. Anxiety has that effect on me."

Oh, not exactly a cause for celebration then. "I'm sorry. I'm sure everything will work out."

"I understand Miss Honeywell is a non-starter," he said.

I narrowed my eyes at Raoul. *You weren't supposed to say anything yet.*

Raoul pointed to Bonkers who was on the scratching post. *It wasn't me.*

I shook my head and crossed the room to my altar where I had everything set up for tonight's spell. Under normal circumstances, I might've consulted Wren or Marigold for the best spell to cast, but my tutors were no longer an option, so I'd done the research myself.

"Why are you enchanting a sweater?" Marley asked as she descended the staircase.

"It isn't a sweater." I held up the knitted material. "It's a shawl."

"Okay, why are you enchanting a shawl?"

"It's going to be my invisibility cloak," I said.

"Can't you do that spell where you keep an enchanted stone in your hand when you want to be invisible?"

"I could if I remembered how to do it, but the shawl will have the added benefit of keeping me warm while I wait."

She joined me at the altar. "Wait where?"

"I'm sneaking over to the Council of Elders meeting tonight to talk to Arthur Rutledge and I don't want to be seen."

"Incredibly, this all makes sense now." Marley touched the shawl. "Do you need help?"

"Thanks. I can manage."

"Does this mean you'll be out late?" she asked.

I listened for any note of distress but there was none.

"No, I'm only going toward the end so I can catch him as he leaves, then I'll come straight home. Promise."

"You'd better hope Aunt Hyacinth doesn't see you. She might think you're there to cause trouble."

"Cause trouble how? Ring a bell outside the cave and shout 'shame' over and over?" Having said that, it occurred to me that it wasn't the worst idea in the world.

"What if she's telling the council members her reasons for shunning us?" Marley asked.

"She wouldn't give them the real reasons. They'd only make her look bad."

"I know," Marley said, "which means she'd tell them a story to make you look bad instead."

I tapped the open page of the book. Marley was right. Aunt Hyacinth was going to play politics and I was letting her.

"I don't care," I finally said. "Let her say whatever wants. If they're willing to believe the lies, that's on them."

Marley nodded solemnly. "That's what I've been telling myself at school."

I focused on her. "What kind of lies are they spreading about you?"

She plucked one of the shawl's loose threads. "That Aunt Hyacinth disowned us because we weren't good enough at magic and we were ruining the family's reputation."

"That one's easy enough to refute. All you need to do is show off your skills in class."

"They're also saying you're not the real niece—that you're an imposter—which means I'm not actually a Rose."

I shrugged. "Would it be so awful to discover we're not actually related to them?"

"Mom, please don't minimize what's happening to me."

I kissed the top of her head. "You're right. I'm sorry. It matters."

I remembered what school was like at her age. No one wanted to be the focus of rumors or ridicule. Marley was still relatively new to the Black Cloak Academy and wouldn't have had time to build a foundation to withstand the intense scrutiny of her classmates.

"Why do you need to speak to Arthur Rutledge in private?" she asked.

"It's about the case I'm working on."

"The one about Granger's dad?"

"Yes."

"I'm glad you're trying to solve his murder. Their family deserves to know what really happened." She fixed her blue eyes on me. "It's one thing we never had to deal with. We know what happened to my dad."

"I think it will help the healing process." The uncertainty had to have been torture for the Nash family. An accident was hard enough to accept, but knowing that Roy's killer walked free...That had to sting each and every day, especially for the sheriff.

"I'll let you finish your spell," Marley said. "I have to study for a quiz before bed."

"Anything I can help with?" I offered.

"I don't think algebra is your strong suit."

"True. Let me know when you get to the unit on cocktail measurements. I'm a pro at that one."

She laughed. "Good luck tonight."

"Thanks," I said. I definitely needed it.

I finished the spell and waited an hour before making my way to the cave where the Council of Elders were mid-meeting. I could hear Mervin O'Malley's raucous laughter from outside and wondered what had pushed the leprechaun's happy button. Maybe Mr. Collins had relayed the story of my embarrassing interview.

I kept myself covered by the enchanted shawl in case anyone left the meeting unexpectedly. I hoped they finished soon because my bladder was going to betray me. I shouldn't have had that extra glass of wine before I left but I needed the liquid courage. Although I didn't want to risk running into Aunt Hyacinth, this was the best way to catch Arthur by surprise and without an audience. I didn't want to give him any time to prepare answers.

My breathing hitched when I spotted Aunt Hyacinth exit the cave, deep in conversation with Victorine Del Bianco, the representative vampire. I was pleased to note that my aunt's face appeared tired and worn, as though she hadn't slept well. Payback. I listened intently in case Marley was right and I was the target of a smear campaign.

"My azaleas aren't blooming," I heard my aunt say and I immediately relaxed.

Arthur was the last to emerge. I lowered the shawl before

he could shift and called his name. The older werewolf turned toward me, a look of surprise on his face.

"Ember, is that you?"

I stepped out of the shadows. "It is. I was hoping to speak with you privately."

He looked around awkwardly. "Here?"

I offered a friendly smile intended to put him at ease. "Why not?"

"If this is about the matter between you and your aunt, I have no interest in getting involved."

"It isn't. I'd like to talk to you about another matter. The murder of Roy Nash."

Deep frown lines creased his forehead. "Roy Nash? Why in the goddess's name would you want to talk to me about that?"

"Because your name is on the original suspect list and I'm revisiting the case."

Arthur glowered at me. "I didn't belong on the list then and I certainly don't belong on it now. Roy Nash was a friend. His death hit the pack very hard."

"According to the file, you and Roy weren't on speaking terms at the time of his death. Something to do with the pack?"

Arthur's nostrils flared. "It isn't a time I wish to revisit."

I forged ahead. "Would you mind telling me what the disagreement was about?"

Arthur studied me for a moment. "I suppose this is how you've decided to occupy your time now that you've lost your position at the newspaper."

"Yes. The sheriff hired me to investigate."

"Is that so?" Arthur seemed to mull it over. "Fine, I'll indulge you out of respect for Sheriff Nash. Roy and I disagreed over my punishment of a young wolf. He was close with the pup's family and thought I was too hard on the boy."

"What did the boy do?" I asked.

Arthur licked his lips. "He was acting out. Took fights with his peers too far. It was causing trouble with a lot of the other youngsters, so I taught him a lesson."

"Taught him how?"

"I used the strap to convince him not to step out of line again," Arthur said.

"The boys' parents didn't object?"

"They were at a loss on how to enforce good behavior, so I stepped in. Successfully, I might add. Too bad Roy died before he could see the end result."

"Why did Roy care?"

"He didn't believe in corporal punishment and wanted the pack to stop using what he referred to as 'violent means' to punish violent actions. I used the strap anyway and Roy refused to speak to me afterward." Arthur hung his head. "One of my greatest regrets is that we ended on bad terms."

"It says you had an alibi for the time of the murder, but the name of the alibi has been blacked out," I said. "Granger's notes say that, when he asked you about it, you couldn't remember. I find it hard to believe you'd forget a thing like that, given that the event is connected to one of the greatest regrets of your life."

Arthur's face grew pinched. "The name was redacted to protect the innocent. In fact, your aunt supplied the spell to keep the name from ever being revealed."

"Why? Who was it?"

"A minor at the time. Beau Hickok," he said.

The air seemed to leave my lungs. "Betty's son?"

He nodded. "The very one who got the strap."

"Why was he with you?"

"He was having a hard time in general. After I doled out his punishment, he changed his tune completely. He seemed to find new respect for me. He began to view me as a confidante. I know you might not understand that, but werewolves…We're not the same as witches and wizards."

My thoughts momentarily flickered to Sheriff Nash. I knew without a doubt that he would've approached Beau's violence with the same reservations as his father.

"One more question, if you don't mind," I said. "I know you can't divulge any secrets from the council meeting, but did my aunt happen to mention me?"

The werewolf shook his head. "Not once."

That was a relief.

"I'm glad someone's taken the torch in the Nash investigation," he continued. "It's been a dark cloud over the head of local werewolves since it happened. It would be wonderful to have a resolution after all this time."

I offered a rueful smile. "Well, don't get too excited. I haven't made much progress."

He gave me a half-hearted pat on the arm. "You've proven yourself a skilled reporter, Ember. I have no doubt you'll be able to dig up new information if there's any to uncover."

"Thanks for the vote of confidence. I'll let you get home. I've taken up enough of your time."

He glanced around the darkened forest. "I'd like to shift and run home if it's all the same to you."

"Go for it." I had no desire to see the wrinkled body of Arthur Rutledge in any form, so I pulled the shawl over my shoulders and made myself scarce.

CHAPTER THIRTEEN

I WOKE up the next morning eager to track down Beau Hickok. It bothered me that the handsome werewolf hadn't felt the need to mention his role as Arthur Rutledge's alibi. Maybe he believed it was no longer relevant, but I would've preferred that he'd been forthcoming. After all, Beau wasn't a minor anymore and Arthur wasn't a suspect. There was no need to hide the information—or was there?

It wasn't hard to find him. One call to Delphine Winter, town librarian and all-around knowledgeable witch, revealed that Beau rented a workspace not far from the Black Cloak Academy.

"So does this mean you're speaking to me?" I asked Delphine. I'd been worried that the witch would hang up when she heard my voice.

"Of course I am," Delphine said.

I paused. "Is that because I'm calling on the phone and no one actually knows you're talking to me?"

Her hesitation was the only answer I needed. "If you come into the library, I'll help you just as I would any other patron."

"But…" I prompted.

"But I'm aware that Hyacinth doesn't want you to be given any special treatment."

"You're aware because she told you this directly?" I asked. I wanted to know exactly what my aunt was saying to members of the coven.

"Not exactly. Listen, Ember. You and I are friends. Your problems with your aunt don't change that." She drew a deep breath. "I just don't want to lose my job, too."

"I appreciate your honesty," I said. I wasn't really surprised. Delphine was far too sweet to stand up to Aunt Hyacinth.

"While I have you on the phone, though," Delphine lowered her voice, "I happen to know there's a job opening at Sunshine Travel, but you didn't hear it from me."

A travel agency sounded promising. "Thanks for the tip. I appreciate it."

I decided not to wait in case the position was close to being filled. I hung up with Delphine and immediately called Sunshine Travel. As luck would have it, the owner was finishing his interviews today so I managed to snag a slot. I'd have to go straight from Beau Hickok to the interview, but I could make it work. I'd just have to wear something a little more professional than I'd planned.

Half an hour later, I parallel-parked on the street in town and meandered toward the workshop, checking the shop windows along the way for any more signs of employment. The workshop was nestled between a hardware store and a bakery. It was probably a good thing the bakery wasn't hiring. I didn't need an extra ten pounds to add to my misery.

I peered inside the workshop window and spied a lone figure hunched over a wooden table. I opened the door and Beau jumped at the sound.

"Sorry, I didn't mean to startle you," I said.

The werewolf cracked a smile. "It's okay. I don't usually get company here. My workplace is kind of my sanctuary."

I noticed the shape of the piece of wood on the table. "Do you make wands?"

He flashed a pair of deep dimples. "I know. Crazy, right? What's a werewolf like me doing with a job like this?"

"It's not crazy at all."

"I started whittling when I was a teenager and I got really good at it. Felt good to keep my hands and brain occupied." He smiled again. "Kept me out of trouble."

I examined the wand on the table. There were three intricate symbols carved into the handle.

"You do beautiful work," I said.

He blushed, which only made him appear more attractive. "Thank you. I love what I do. I know not everyone can say that."

"No, definitely not." I knew that all too well. After coming to Starry Hollow, I'd hoped to never have to work a job I hated again.

"Want a woodworking lesson?" Beau asked. "I can show you how skilled I am with my hands." He wiggled his fingers suggestively.

"Maybe another time," I said. "I'm here to talk to you about Roy Nash's murder."

He frowned. "Didn't you already speak to my mom?"

"I did, but I've learned a few bits of information since then, one of which involves you."

Beau made a face. "Rutledge."

"That's right. He said my aunt is actually the witch who magically redacted your name to protect your identity."

"I was a minor and the pack was worried I'd get dragged into nasty adult business." Beau fiddled with the wand on the table. "Rutledge is actually the one who got me into woodworking. He wanted me to find a way to channel my energy into something productive."

I reached for the wand. "May I?"

Beau nodded. "Be my guest. It's for a witch's hand, after all."

I held the wand in my hand and rubbed the grooves of the symbols with my thumb. "Did Arthur encourage you to make wands?"

He chuckled. "Nope. That came as a surprise to everyone. They thought I'd make more rugged things like tables and chairs, but I like the delicate yet powerful nature of wands."

I aimed the wand at the far wall, pretending to cast a spell. "What do the other wolves think of your livelihood?"

"You know how werewolves are. Jayce accuses me of selling out and betraying my kind. Some of the guys ask if I've carved myself a…" He glanced down at his waist. "Werewolves can be merciless."

"Can you tell me more about the evening of the murder? What were you doing with Arthur Rutledge?"

Beau wore a faraway look. "We had a woodworking lesson, then he took me to dinner. Burgers and shakes at the diner. I was going through a hard time. Lots of anger. My parents were bickering a lot, which didn't help."

"What were you angry about?"

"In hindsight, I think it was partly hormones and partly family drama. I'm glad Arthur took me under his wing. I needed an authority figure to set me straight and put me on a good path. If it weren't for Rutledge, I'd probably be serving a life sentence in prison right now."

I set the wand back on the table. "Was the family drama to do with Roy and your mom?"

He looked pained by the memory. "Yeah. Dad was pissed about a necklace he found hidden in Mom's drawer. Mom seemed to be in tears all the time. It was miserable for all of us."

"Did you believe your mom and Roy were involved in a secret relationship?"

He gave an adamant shake of his head. "No way. We all spent a lot of time together, but that was it."

"Your dad obviously didn't feel that way, at least initially."

"He had a temper," Beau said. "Apparently, he was a real hell raiser when he was younger, but he mellowed when he married my mom. She used to say Jayce and I were karma."

"If that's true, then how do you explain Wyatt?" I asked good-naturedly. By all accounts, Roy was a good guy and always had been.

"Wyatt wasn't so much a hell raiser. He was naturally competitive, but more interested in impressing girls than anything else."

"How would you describe your relationship with the Nash brothers now?"

Beau tapped the wand against his open palm. "Non-existent. I miss those guys, though. We were so close when we were younger."

"Have you tried reaching out?"

"I see Wyatt at the bars sometimes. We don't avoid each other, but we don't make plans to hang out either. I get the impression Granger's too wrapped up in his job for a social life."

"I think he might be open to it," I said.

He looked at me with interest. "You two are friends?"

"We are."

His gaze raked over me. "Exactly how friendly are you?"

I ignored the question. "Did you have any theories about what happened to Roy? Any gossip you remember hearing among the other wolves?"

Beau shook his head. "No. Even if there had been, I was

too wrapped up in my own stuff to notice. I was a teenager, you know? Nothing else was as important as what I was dealing with." He flipped the wand into the air and caught it. "Center of the universe syndrome."

I smiled. "I can think of a few grown men suffering from that affliction."

His dimples made another appearance. "If you'd like to have dinner with a more evolved one, my dance card has room for another name."

I inclined my head toward the wand. "I get the feeling you make notches in more places than a wand."

He laughed. "I'll take that as a no."

"I just got out of a relationship," I admitted. "I don't think dinner with a charming werewolf should be my immediate response."

"If you change your mind, you know where to find me." He grinned. "Just me and my impressive wood."

I groaned and turned toward the door. "See you around, Beau."

I arrived at my interview with five minutes to spare. I tried to clear my mind of the murder investigation so I didn't inadvertently mention the words 'alibi' or 'suspect' during my interview.

"Welcome to Sunshine Travel," the receptionist chirped. I noticed a collection of troll dolls with different colored hair lined up along the edge of the desk.

"Hi, I'm Ember Rose. I'm here for an interview with Mr. Mayhew."

Her bright smile seemed frozen in place. I got the sense that she'd wear the same expression if I'd asked her for directions or a square of toilet paper.

"Terrific. He's ready for you now. Straight back and to the left."

"Thank you."

The walls of Mr. Mayhew's office were lined with vintage-style travel posters. The only name I recognized was Rainbow Falls.

"Welcome to Sunshine Travel," the troll said. "Have a seat."

"Now I understand your receptionist's collection," I said, lowering myself into the chair.

He looked at me blankly. "What do you mean?"

Heat rushed to my cheeks. "Never mind."

"Why don't you tell me about yourself?" he asked.

I tried to adopt a charming smile. "I'm opting for the less-is-more approach."

The troll tilted his head. "I don't understand."

"The less you know about me, the more likely you are to hire me."

His confusion registered. "Ah, interview humor to dispel the tension. How refreshing. Tell me, Miss Rose, what kind of relevant experience do you have?"

"Well, I've helped my cousins Florian and Aster with their work on the tourism board."

He tugged his ear. "Yes, but that's for enticing others to visit Starry Hollow, not for our residents to visit elsewhere."

"You don't think that's relevant?"

He drummed his plump fingers on the edge of the desk. "Not really, no."

Terrific.

"Why don't we try this another way? You can start by telling me why you want this job."

"Because I have a strong aversion to being hungry and homeless."

His brow creased. "I see. And what would you say are your greatest strengths?"

"Juggling lots of responsibilities," I said.

He leaned forward, appearing eager to hear more. "Such as?"

"I've had to jam a lot into a single day. My work…" I laughed awkwardly. "Well, not anymore obviously. Magic lessons…Well, not those either because she banned the tutors from helping me." I didn't want to mention the murder investigation or Arnold Palmer. That left me with— "Um, showering."

His brow lifted. "You consider showering to be a responsibility?"

"If you've ever smelled me after a day without one, you'd understand."

Mr. Mayhew wrinkled his nose. "What are your skills, Miss Rose?"

"Hmm. Skills. Let's see?" I tapped my foot, trying to remember the answers I'd practiced in my head earlier, but my mind went blank. "I can use almost all the buttons on the microwave. Even the ones no one knows like the melting feature." I folded my arms proudly.

"There's a melting feature?"

"Exactly."

"What about skills related to the job?" he asked.

I struggled to think of an answer. "I can use the microwave in the break room. Show everyone else how to use it." Ugh, this was a colossal waste of time. I shouldn't have bothered.

"Where do you envision yourself in five years?" Mr. Mayhew asked.

"I guess that depends on a few factors," I said. "Marley will be preparing to leave for college and I'll be on my own for the first time ever. I was still in high school myself when she was born." I paused. "Maybe I shouldn't have mentioned that. Anyway, if my aunt and I are still at odds, then I'll probably rent out the cottage and move somewhere else. I don't want to sell it because it belonged to my parents and they're both dead now…"

He cleared his throat. "I mean in reference to your career, Miss Rose."

I laughed. "Oh, right. That makes more sense. I would like to be doing a job I enjoy and earning a living without worrying about paying the bills."

"And where's your favorite paranormal spot to visit?" he asked.

It suddenly occurred to me that I'd only been to one. "Spellbound."

He lit up at the mention of the famous cursed town. "I haven't been yet, but it's on my bucket list. Where else?"

"Um, that's it."

"Oh." He steepled his fingers. "You don't like to travel?"

"It's not that. I'm a single mom, so I don't have the luxury of taking off whenever the mood strikes me. I'm from the human world. Does that count?"

"Interesting. From anywhere good?"

I bit my lip. "Define good."

"Detroit, Michigan?" he ventured.

Okay, not the answer I was expecting. "No, I'm from New Jersey."

He winced. "I'm sorry."

I wagged a finger. "Now *that* answer I was expecting."

"How are your interpersonal skills? Do you get along well with others?"

I shifted uncomfortably in the chair. "Define 'well.'"

"Part of this job involves getting on well with customers and being in tune with their wants and needs."

I wasn't even in tune with the wants and needs of a houseplant. "Can there be alcohol involved?"

Mr. Mayhew shuffled papers around his desk and I could see he'd ruled me out. My spirits deflated. It was like Lucy letting the air out of the football instead of yanking away the ball before Charlie Brown could kick it.

"You're not going to hire me, are you?" I asked.

Mr. Mayhew offered a sympathetic grunt. "I'm afraid not, Miss Rose."

I slung the strap of my purse over my shoulder and stood. "Would you happen to have any suggestions for where else I might look? I'm not seeing many ads for jobs I'm qualified for."

"No, I suppose you wouldn't," he said.

Wow. Way to kick me when I'm down.

"You might want to do a bit of soul-searching," he continued. "Figure out what your skills are and where they might be put to good use. I have to believe you're capable of more than manning a microwave."

He was right. I was. A lot more.

"I'm sorry I wasted your time," I said, rising to a standing position.

"I don't believe that anything is a waste of time," he said. "There's a lesson to be learned in our every encounter should we choose to pay attention."

"And what was your lesson from this encounter?" I asked.

"That I should screen my candidates more closely before agreeing to an interview." He folded his hands on the desk. "And what was yours?"

I smiled. "Same."

I'd gotten nowhere with the murder investigation and nowhere with the job hunt, so I decided to take another stab at matchmaking. If I continued to knock on doors of opportunity, I had to believe that one would eventually open. Raoul had turned up a location for the third and final prospect for Arnold Palmer, so we arranged to interview her together.

According to Raoul's source, Lavender Soap was the proud owner of—wait for it—an eponymous handmade soap company. We found her workshop tucked away down a side alley of Potions Lane.

I pushed open the door and was immediately assaulted by a variety of competing scents. Lavender, chamomile, rose, vanilla—there were too many to identify in one sniff. The rustic space included multiple wooden worktables and a large farmhouse sink.

"This smells like Haverford House," I said.

Yeah, it definitely has that old lady smell, Raoul said.

I gently smacked his back. "Don't insult Artemis. She's the sweetest witch in all of Starry Hollow."

Only because she's too forgetful to remember to be mean.

"Hello?" A head popped up from behind a counter. The witch's hair was blond with lavender tips and purple eyeshadow covered her eyelids.

"Hi, we're looking for Lavender Soap," I said.

"You're looking at her," the witch said. She bustled to a nearby table, carrying a tray of soap samples.

"I'm Ember Rose and this is my familiar, Raoul."

He nudged me. *Tell her I'm your associate. It's more legit.*

Her gaze shifted to the raccoon. "This is your familiar?"

Uh oh. Were we going to have a repeat of Laurel Honeywell?

"Yes. This is a nice business you have here," I said. "I think I've seen your soaps in some of the local shops."

"I'm sure you have. I sell to just about everybody," the witch said. "I wasn't interested in running my own shop on top of making the soap." She removed the samples from the tray and set them in a line on the table.

"We're here because we represent Arnold Palmer, one of your potential familiars," I explained.

"Arnold Palmer?" She appeared thoughtful. "Oh, right. I've been so busy that I've barely had time to look over the information the agency sent me."

Lavender hustled back to the sink where she washed her hands.

"Do you ever stop moving?" I asked good-naturedly. She reminded me of people in New Jersey who seemed to be in a constant state of motion.

Lavender wiped her wet hands on a towel. "I'm a busy witch, Miss Rose. My familiar will find that out soon enough."

Raoul tugged on the hem of my suit jacket. *Ask her about leisure time.*

"What are your interests?" I asked.

She glanced up at me with a quizzical expression. "What do you mean?"

"Do you like to read? Do crossword puzzles? Fly on a broomstick?"

"Who has time for that?" she scoffed. "I make soap. I sell soap. I go home, make dinner, have a bubble bath, and go to bed."

"There's no one special waiting at home for you?" I suspected I already knew the answer. If Lavender didn't have time to read a few pages of a book each night, she likely didn't make the time for someone special.

"I hope my familiar will take on that role." She began wrapping soap bars in beautiful sheets of paper and tying them with lavender ribbons. "Of course, I'll expect them to help me with making soap."

"You could just hire an assistant," I suggested.

I'm working with you, Raoul said. *Why shouldn't Arnold help make soap?*

It's not the same, I said.

I feel like you're looking for reasons to discount her.

Maybe he was right. I was still stuck on Violet for some reason, despite our disappointing meeting with her. There was something about the witch that spoke to me.

Lavender bent down to sniff one of the bars of soap before she wrapped it. "Look, I know the qualities I want in a familiar and if I can't find one who ticks the boxes, then I'm content to leave it be."

"Why apply for a familiar at all?" I asked. "You seem happy with the way things are."

Lavender surveyed her wrapped soaps. "It gets so tiring. Every family function, one of my relatives inevitably asks 'so when are you going to get a familiar?' 'Any plans to add to the family?'" She groaned. "I just want to put an end to the questions and comments."

"That's not really the best reason to commit to another living creature, is it?" I asked.

Lavender shrugged. "Paranormals have been motivated by lesser reasons."

"Arnold Palmer would make any witch a lovely familiar," I said. "I think he deserves to be with a witch who appreciates him and genuinely wants the relationship."

The witch glanced at Raoul and back to me. "How would you describe your relationship? I guess you two get along pretty well if you're willing to work together."

"We do. He's easy to please. A little trash on occasion and a weekly pizza and he's eternally devoted."

I'm not THAT easy, he grumbled.

Lavender seemed to mull it over. "This familiar—Arnold—he's nice, you say?"

"Very nice. Extremely polite. An asset to any witch."

She nodded. "Then I think I should remove myself from contention. He sounds like he deserves better than what I can offer him."

Well, that wasn't the outcome I was expecting.

See? You chased her away. Now what?

I kept my focus on Lavender. "I appreciate your candor," I said. "I'll be sure to let my client know."

"And I'll alert the agency." The witch frowned. "I know it's not my concern, but what will he do if he doesn't find a match?"

My thoughts flicked to Violet's messy garden and her disheveled kitchen.

"Don't worry, Lavender. I have a feeling Arnold Palmer is going to be just fine."

CHAPTER FOURTEEN

I RETURNED to Rose Cottage and rifled through the contents of the sheriff's box, looking for another loose thread I could pull. My gaze landed on the sheriff's notes—Missing File A. If I was going to leave no stone unturned, then that meant finding the elusive file.

"Raoul, I need a town map," I called. He'd gone straight into the kitchen when we arrived home and I hadn't seen him since.

"I believe Raoul has gone for a walk in the woods, but I can fetch one for you, miss," Arnold Palmer said.

I'd been so engrossed in the files, I hadn't even noticed that the pink fairy armadillo was in the cottage.

"Thank you," I said, gathering ingredients for the locator spell. "Did he tell you about Lavender Soap?"

The armadillo lowered his head. "He did, miss. I'd say it's probably for the best."

I was inclined to agree. Even though Lavender seemed like a decent witch, she wasn't the right match for Arnold Palmer.

He fluttered over to the table a few minutes later with a

folded map and I opened it in the center of the table. If the file had been deliberately hidden the way Beau's name had been magically redacted, then I might not be able to find it using a spell, but it was worth a try.

I sprinkled the spelled herbs across the map and placed my hands on top. Closing my eyes, I performed the incantation exactly as it was written in the book. Power flowed through my body and I felt Ivy's magic entwined with my own. It was strange how I could still sense each strand of magic, as though they could still be separated.

When I opened my eyes, an 'X' had formed on the map. It was only when I looked closer that I recognized the location—the missing file was at the sheriff's office. I brushed the spelled herbs off the map and tucked them inside an amulet. I clasped the chain around my neck and hurried to the car. If the file was still in the sheriff's office, then it had likely been misplaced years ago.

Deputy Bolan was in the lobby when I arrived. He rolled his little leprechaun eyes when he spotted me hurrying toward him.

"There's a public restroom around the corner," he said. "No need to come barging in here."

I glared at him. "I don't need the bathroom." Well, I did now that he'd mentioned it, but I wouldn't give him the satisfaction.

"Then what is it now, Rose? I know you're not working on any articles."

"No, I'm looking for a missing file in connection with Roy Nash's murder. According to the spell I just cast, it's somewhere in this office."

"And I suppose you'd like to poke around without an escort and treat the hub of law enforcement like it's your personal playground?"

"Of course not. If this were my personal playground, there'd be a bar right over there." I pointed to the front desk.

The deputy begrudgingly waved me forward. I passed the front desk and concentrated on the amulet. It lifted away from my chest, indicating that I should walk straight on. It tugged me along the corridor, all the way to one of the storage rooms. Maybe the file had simply been placed in the wrong box.

The deputy looked at me. "I suppose you need me to unlock the storage room."

"That would save me from doing another spell," I said. "I'm doing this for the sheriff, you know."

Deputy Bolan used a key on his chain to unlock the door. "I know. Why do you think I'm helping you at all?"

The door swung open and the amulet immediately reacted. It tugged me toward the left. The storage room was located in the older part of the building and it showed. The floorboards were the original oak with wide planks and a little more dust than I would have expected in the sheriff's office. I watched the amulet closely for my next move. It shot straight out and then yanked downward so hard that it pulled a muscle in my neck.

"Ouch," I said, rubbing the injury.

I glanced around, uncertain. There were shelves of boxes on either side of me, but the amulet didn't seem to indicate left or right. I moved to the left and gauged the amulet's response. It pulled me back to the middle. I shifted to the right with the same results. I looked down at the floor, frowning.

"Is there a basement?" I asked.

"No. There's nothing underneath here except the foundation of the building," the deputy said.

I shifted to my knees and noticed a small gap between two of the floorboards. It wasn't so wide that I noticed it from a standing position, but I could see it clearly now. More importantly, it was wide enough for a thin file to slip through.

I twisted to look at the leprechaun. "I need to remove these floorboards. Can you help me?"

"I think we'll need permission to do a thing like that."

"Are you seriously going to make me jump through bureaucratic hoops to find this missing file?" I asked. "What if this is the answer that we've been looking for? What if this file reveals the killer of Granger's dad?"

Deputy Bolan only hesitated for a moment before acquiescing. "I'm a busy officer of the law. I'm not getting any tools."

I rubbed my hands together. "I've got tools right here."

He peered over my shoulder. "You're talking about your magic hands, right?"

I craned my neck to look at him. "As opposed to what? My magic boobs?"

"I don't know," he said, exasperated. "Neither one is in my wheelhouse."

I let the magic flow to my fingertips and focused on the floorboards. "*Relegare*," I said.

The floorboard shifted and I peered through the gap. A sliver of color where no color should be caught my eye. My pulse sped up.

"It's here," I said. "I need your little fingers." Bolan's fingers were like tiny crab pincers.

The deputy scowled but kneeled beside me and dipped his hand through the gap to retrieve the file. It was layered in dust and we both coughed as he handed it to me.

"Satisfied?" he asked.

"Very." Two successful spells in a row. My tutors would be proud. Too bad I wasn't able to share my accomplishments.

I brushed away the dust and opened the file.

Deputy Bolan crossed his arms. "Well, what's the big reveal? I bet it's a blank file that nobody used."

My throat went dry. "You guessed right." I snapped the file closed.

He gave me a strange look. "Then why does your expression suggest otherwise?"

I resumed a standing position and clutched the file to my chest. No way was I sharing this information with Deputy Bolan, not until I knew more.

"I'm just stunned that I managed to remove the floorboard."

He gestured to the shifted board. "You need to put it back now. I'm not going to be responsible for any mess."

I put everything as it was and tucked the file under my arm. Wordlessly, I fled the office and returned to my car where I opened the file for a second look, just to be sure my eyes hadn't deceived me. My stomach curdled as I read the name at the top of the page.

Alec Hale.

Alec was exactly where I expected him to be—alone in his office at *Vox Populi*. The vampire was a creature of habit and a breakup with me wasn't going to rock his world enough to change that. In fact, the end of our relationship would probably only serve to strengthen his routine.

Thankfully, Bentley and Tanya were gone for the day. This wasn't a conversation I'd want either of them to overhear.

The door to Alec's office was ajar. As usual, the vampire was fixated on the screen of his laptop. He glanced up, his surprise registering.

"Ember, I didn't expect to see you here."

"I didn't expect to be here, but there's something I need to ask you."

He motioned to the empty chair in front of the desk. "You look well."

"I look like crap, but I appreciate the lie." Looking at him now, I realized that he didn't look too great either.

"Why are you in a suit?" he asked. "Ah, it's the monthly coven meeting tonight, isn't it?"

"Yes," I said. Inwardly, I groaned. I'd completely forgotten that was tonight. Maybe I'd skip this month.

"Everyone here misses you," he said.

I arched an eyebrow. "Everyone?"

"Yes, of course," he said simply. "I'm working on edits this evening. I let them pile up and now I'm paying the price."

I grimaced. "I'm sorry. I know how much you hate the editing process."

He closed the lid of his laptop. "If you're here about a reference, I can ask Tanya tomorrow…"

"No, I'm not here about a reference, but thank you." My fingers tightened around the handle of the tote bag. "I've been working on Roy Nash's case since Bentley abandoned ship."

"I see. I suppose Sheriff Nash appreciates your interest."

"This isn't about the sheriff. This is about what I found." I tossed the missing file onto his desk. "Can you explain this?"

Alec opened the file and reviewed the contents. "Yes, of course. I remember being questioned about this."

My eyes popped. "Alec, this isn't a pleasant trip down memory lane. You were a suspect in the murder of Granger's dad."

"Only for about five seconds until they came to their senses."

"How could you not have mentioned this to me?"

"Why would I?" He seemed genuinely perplexed. "It was a

non-issue as far as I was concerned. They ruled me out quickly and I thought no more of it. I'm surprised there's a file. That's how inconsequential it was."

"Why did they suspect you?" I asked.

He lifted the file. "I'm going to assume you've read this."

"Yes, but I want to hear your version of events."

"There's no version of events, Ember. What it says here is accurate. Roy Nash and I were seen quarreling the week before he died."

"Before he was murdered," I corrected him. "What did you fight about?"

He dragged a hand through his dark blond hair. "I was writing an article for the newspaper about local corruption and a few members of the werewolf pack were named in it."

"Was Roy one of them?"

"No, certainly not. His reputation was pristine."

"Then why was he involved?"

"He worried about the pack's reputation and believed the allegations were unfounded. He saw me in the pub and decided to take up the matter with me right there and then."

"Were the allegations unfounded?" I pressed.

"Of course not. I wouldn't dream of printing an article without factual support. You know that."

I did know that. "Did you share the evidence with him?"

"I couldn't. I had to protect my sources. He was convinced I was out to ruin families and tear the pack apart, which is ridiculous."

"Was the pack all one unit then?" The werewolves in town weren't as organized as the coven. They seemed to function as many different factions rather than one large pack.

"More or less," Alec said. "The corruption splintered the group, or at least widened the gaps that already existed."

"Which is what Roy was afraid of."

"I didn't create the corruption, Ember. I only reported it."

"What was the corruption?" I asked.

Alec drummed his fingers on the desk, appearing to think. "Kickbacks. Nepotism. Bribery."

I whistled. "Sounds like a mess."

"Your aunt wasn't very popular at the time either. She threw her weight around to make sure that all the guilty parties were removed from power."

I thought about the chip on Sheriff Nash's shoulder when it came to my aunt and wondered whether he'd been influenced by these events as a youth. If he only heard the werewolves' side of it and saw the negative repercussions for the pack, I could understand how it might've shaped his view.

"I don't suppose you and Hyacinth have reconciled," he continued.

"No, and I don't see that happening anytime soon."

"I'm sorry to hear it, though I don't suppose you'd return here either way."

"I don't think that would be wise under the circumstances. In fact, I've been interviewing for jobs," I said.

Alec observed me closely. "And how is that going?"

I offered an embarrassed smile. "It isn't. Turns out I'm not fit for very much."

"Don't underestimate yourself. You're the most capable paranormal I know."

We stared at each other for a long moment. I was acutely aware of the beating of my heart and knew the vampire must be, too. Alec broke the silence first.

"It was wonderful to see you." He returned the file to me. "I'm sorry I didn't think to mention this before. To be honest, I barely remember it."

"Then you didn't make sure the file went missing?"

His laughter was a mixture of shock and amusement. "Don't you think if I wanted a file to disappear that I would've destroyed it?"

He was right. The likelihood was that the file had been unknowingly dropped on its way to the storage box and left to rot.

"I had no reason to keep this from you," he said, his voice softening. "The sheriff ruled me out for lack of evidence."

"Did you have an alibi for the evening of his murder?"

"I did, as a matter of fact. I was in New York meeting with my agent and publisher. The sheriff substantiated it. If you'd like to do it again, I won't stop you. I'll even make the call myself if it will help."

"That won't be necessary." I believed him. As flawed as he was, Alec had never lied to me. I saw no reason he'd start now.

"I'm glad you're keeping busy."

"It helps not to be in my own head for too long." I tucked the file into my tote bag and rose to my feet. "I'm sorry to interrupt your edits, but I had to ask."

"I understand." His gaze lingered on me. "Tell Marley hello for me. It isn't the same without her. Without either of you."

A lump formed in my throat and I couldn't bring myself to respond.

"Are we to be friends, do you think?" he asked.

"Not today." I looped the strap over my shoulder. "But maybe someday." I turned and headed for the doorway.

"I hope so," he said quietly.

I refused to look back. I knew if I did that I'd do something foolish, so I did the only reasonable thing I could. I looked straight ahead and kept going.

CHAPTER FIFTEEN

"Do I look presentable?" I asked. I smoothed the front of my dress and examined my reflection in the mirror. As tempted as I was to skip the monthly coven meeting, I knew it wasn't the right thing to do.

"Are you sure you want to wear red?" Marley asked. She sat cross-legged on my bed, observing me with a concerned expression. "I feel like you're making a point if you wear red."

I ran a brush through my hair one more time to tame the frizz. "Maybe I am."

"You don't have to go," Marley said. "You and I can have our own meeting here at the cottage. I'll whip up Wish cookies to make it seem realistic."

"I'm not letting her bully me," I said. "Silver Moon is my coven, too, and I have every right to be there." I also felt it was necessary to lead my daughter by example. If I avoided uncomfortable moments, then what was to stop her from staying home from school to do the same?

"Okay, but try not to make eye contact," Marley said. "She might take it as a personal insult."

I met my daughter's gaze in the reflection. "She can take it however she likes. I'll make a few adjustments like sitting at the opposite end of the table, but I'm not altering my behavior just to avoid a confrontation."

"The teacher moved my seat, but it hasn't helped."

I frowned. "Why would she move your seat? You're not the one causing trouble in class."

Marley shrugged. "Because it's easier to move one seat than three, I guess."

I whirled around to face her. "Marley Rose, I don't like this one bit. Let me get involved."

"No, absolutely not. You're dealing with enough right now." She slid her feet to the floor. "Good luck tonight. I hope it's painless."

"Well, we know it won't be that, but I'll survive." After all, I'd survived much worse.

I swiped my purse off the bed before heading downstairs with Marley following closely behind.

"My homework is done, so I'll just read a chapter before bed," she said.

I stopped in the living room and turned to face her. "Are you sure you don't want me to find someone else to stay?" As my aunt's employee, Mrs. Babcock was now off-limits as a sitter for Marley and my cousins would be attending the meeting with me.

Marley squared her shoulders. "I'll be fine. I want to get a good night's sleep for school tomorrow. I have a feeling we're getting a pop quiz in math."

I stroked her hair. "You're growing up so fast. Where did the time go?"

She wrapped her arms around my waist. "Don't worry. Everything will work out."

I gave her a squeeze and released her. "Maybe say a little prayer to the gods before bed. No harm in asking."

I grabbed my cloak and patted PP3 on the head on my

way out. As soon as I slid behind the wheel of the car, I cranked up the volume of *My Life* by Billy Joel to boost my spirits and sped off toward coven headquarters.

I parked the car and checked my phone for messages. I had an encouraging text from Florian and one from Linnea to tell me that she'd saved me a seat next to her. It felt strange not to have one from Alec. Despite his flaws, he was supportive—except for that time he fired me because my aunt demanded it. And when he refused to try to work through his issues to improve our relationship.

So maybe not as supportive as I'd wanted to believe.

Naturally the room was packed tonight. It almost felt personal, as though the whole coven knew about the feud and turned up to watch the drama unfold. Well, I wouldn't be putting on a show for anyone. I was here to participate as a member of the coven and that was it.

I spotted the back of Aunt Hyacinth's head. She sat at the front as expected, chatting with Iris Sandstone, the High Priestess. As I approached the table, Iris's gaze flicked to me and then back to my aunt. I was relieved to see that her expression remained neutral. If the High Priestess decided to take sides, I knew which one she'd choose and it wasn't the side of the relative newcomer.

I joined Linnea at the far end of the table. My cousin leaned over and hugged me. I knew she was making a point to anyone watching and I loved her all the more for it.

"I guess I haven't missed anything," I whispered.

"Just the snacks and pre-meeting chitchat. We're about to start."

Florian gave me subtle salute and Aster smiled. Aunt Hyacinth kept her back turned toward the front throughout the meeting. I listened with half an ear as the various coven officials went through the agenda. The bake sale brought in more money than expected thanks to muffins that accidentally included a sleep-inducing herb. There were apparently many well-rested individuals last month.

Under new business, there was a discussion as to whether the coven carnival should change locations this year, followed by a periodic reminder to update wills and living wills.

Aunt Hyacinth rose to her feet. "I can highly recommend my own lawyer should you be in need of one. I recently updated my will and the firm did a superb job as always. Very knowledgeable and efficient." She gave me a pointed look over her shoulder as she returned to her seat.

I felt like I'd been punched in the stomach. Linnea patted my leg under the table.

"Never mind her," she whispered. "She's just trying to assert her dominance in front of everyone. I bet she didn't really change her will."

"I don't want her money," I said. I'd managed without it this long. There was no need to lament an imaginary loss.

"Mother plans to live forever anyway," Linnea said with a smile. "I doubt any of us will ever see a single coin."

Once the meeting ended, I bolted for the door. I felt everyone's pitying eyes on me and I wanted to escape as quickly as possible. It had been a mistake to come and pretend everything was normal. It was too far from it.

Wren Stanton-Summer intercepted me before I could cross the threshold to freedom. "You're not staying for cookies?" the wizard asked. "That isn't like you."

"I made it through the meeting. That feels like enough of an accomplishment for one evening."

The wizard regarded me with a mixture of guilt and sympathy. "I'm sorry about our lessons."

"Not sorry enough to disregard my aunt's instructions," I shot back. Standing in front of him now, I realized how hurt I truly was that my tutors had abandoned me.

Wren winced. "She's the one who ordered the lessons in the first place. They were hers to cancel."

"You didn't give me the option of continuing," I said. "Maybe I would've paid you out of my town pocket."

Wren placed a hand on my arm. "I'm sorry, Ember. We all are. Nobody wants to get on the wrong side of Hyacinth, though. It's coven suicide. Surely you can understand that."

I looked him directly in the eye. "Maybe it's me you should be worried about."

I brushed past him and pushed open the door, filling my lungs with the crisp night air as I hurried to the parking lot. It was only when I was safely ensconced in my car that I let the emotional dam burst. Tears spilled down my cheeks as reality sank in. I'd lost Alec. My aunt. My social standing. Was this how my father had felt when he decided to leave town after my mother's death? My chest tightened as I contemplated how alone he must've felt. At least Marley was practically an adult during my time of strife. I'd only been an infant when my father escaped Starry Hollow and moved to the human world where he knew absolutely no one. No support system. No money.

Gods, he'd been so brave. I never appreciated him more than I did in this moment.

I opened the car door, too shaken up to drive. Maybe a walk would calm the noise in my head before I drove home. I didn't want to return to Marley like this. If she was awake, she'd sense my distress and I didn't want that. I needed her to believe that everything was okay.

I shrugged off my cloak and tossed it onto the passenger seat. Wiping my tears away, I started around the block.

"Twice in one day," a voice said. "Don't I feel lucky?"

I glanced up to see Beau Hickok walking toward me. Beside him was another werewolf, slightly bigger and broader but with the same head of hair and rugged features. Between them, the Hickok brothers and the Nash brothers had to be the most handsome werewolves in town.

"Hello, Beau," I said.

His affable grin widened, putting his dimples on display. "This is my brother, Jayce."

Jayce's handshake was softer than his appearance suggested. "Nice dress," he said.

"Oh, thanks. I just came from a coven meeting."

"Meetings are the worst," Beau said. "Or at least that one must've been based on your expression. I bet you need a drink. Why don't you join us? We're heading to the Wishing Well to meet friends."

The thought of a drink with two handsome strangers was exactly what I needed. These werewolves wouldn't care about Aunt Hyacinth's edicts and mandates, or the fact that she'd written me out of her will. They were as close as I could get to oblivion in Starry Hollow.

"I'd love to," I said.

The moment we entered the Wishing Well, I worried I'd made a mistake. Sheriff Nash stood at the bar, having drinks with Deputy Bolan and Deputy Pitt. He caught my eye and frowned at the sight of a Hickok brother on either side of me.

"Good evening," I greeted them.

"Who's on duty if the three of you are boozing it up here?" Beau asked.

"No one's boozing it up," Deputy Bolan said, indignant. "We're celebrating Deputy Pitt joining the team and I'm toasting with elderflower and water."

"Seems like bad luck to toast without alcohol," Beau said.

"What can I get for you, Ember?" Jayce offered.

"Whatever you order, make sure the glass is filled to the rim or she feels like it's a rip-off," Sheriff Nash said.

I shrugged. "Guilty as charged."

Jayce's gaze darted to me. "Sure thing."

"I see Matty and Leo," Beau said. "They're in a booth over there."

"We'll be over in a second," Jayce said.

"It was the coven meeting tonight, wasn't it?" the sheriff asked.

"Why do you think I'm here now?" I turned and followed Beau to the booth.

Jayce joined us a few minutes later with the first round. Matty and Leo both seemed pleased to be in mixed company.

"How'd you meet these two bozos?" Matty asked.

"Met Jayce tonight and I met Beau at his mother's condo," I said.

Beau ducked his head. "You don't want to know more than that. Trust me."

Leo grinned. "Sounds intriguing."

"Granger seems to know you pretty well," Jayce said to me. "I always liked him."

Beau laughed. "That's because he didn't compete with you like Wyatt did."

Jayce glanced at the sheriff, still at the bar. "I feel bad that we're not close anymore."

Beau nodded. "Yeah, it's weird to spend a big chunk of our childhood with them and now we're practically strangers, but Ember seems to think he'd be open to hanging out with us again."

Jayce waved a dismissive hand. "Nah. His life's too busy now. Whenever I see him around town, he's in uniform."

"He's not in uniform now," I said. I resisted the urge to check out the sheriff's tight jeans.

"But he's with his law enforcement pals," Jayce said.

"I wouldn't mind getting to know the new deputy," Matty said. "Maybe even sample her handcuffs."

Jayce elbowed him. "Watch your gutter mouth when there's a lady present."

"Oh, I'm not a lady," I said. "I'm from New Jersey."

"I wish my mom would move somewhere closer like that," Beau said. "Arizona seems so far."

"Are either of you tempted to move with her?" I asked.

"I've considered it," Jayce said. "I don't have anyone special here, so it might be a good time to shake things up."

Beau swilled his ale. "No way would you ever leave me."

Jayce appeared chagrined. "No, you're right. I guess you'll have to be my someone special."

I couldn't help but smile. The brothers seemed to have a sweet bond. It was a shame Granger and Wyatt were more often at odds, although I understood the reasons. Wyatt was a royal pain with misguided ethics and Granger was his polar opposite.

"I'll miss your mom's short ribs," Leo said.

"I'll miss her sweet potato pie," Jayce said. "I might need to learn to make it myself."

Beau emptied his glass and set it on the table. "I wouldn't object to that."

"I'm trying to learn to cook," I said. "It's been a chink in my parental armor for a long time and I promised my daughter I'd try to remedy that."

"You're a witch," Beau said. "Can't you just do a spell and whip up something delicious?"

"I'm not that adept at cooking or magic," I said. I neglected to mention my influx of power. The revelation that I had more power than skill wasn't something to brag about.

"But you're willing to learn. That's the important thing." Jayce's gaze lingered on me a few seconds longer than necessary and I felt a pleasant shiver in response. Although I wasn't interested in meeting anyone so soon after my breakup, I had to admit the positive attention was nice.

"I'll get the next round," I said.

Matty perked up. "You're a real keeper, aren't you?"

I vacated the booth and joined the sheriff and Deputy Pitt at the bar. "Where's Deputy Bolan?"

"Duty called," Sheriff Nash said. "Looks like you're having a good time."

"It was needed," I admitted. "The coven meeting was harder than expected. I left my car there, so I'll have to go back for it in the morning. Make sure Bolan doesn't give me a ticket."

He chuckled. "Will do. How's Marley?"

I offered a sad smile. "School's also been harder than expected."

Deputy Pitt leaned over. "Oh, are you in school? I had an older woman in my college classes…"

I stiffened. "I'm talking about my daughter."

She looked down at her glass. "Oops, sorry."

The sheriff clapped me on the shoulder. "Rose is a graduate of the School of Hard Knocks."

"Definitely seems like it sometimes," I muttered.

Deputy Pitt glanced at her phone. "Ooh, it's getting late. I should really head home. Don't want to be late for work tomorrow. I hear the boss is a real stickler." She gave him a playful wink.

"I won't be far behind you. Have a good night, Pitt."

"Welcome to the team," I called after her. "She knows I'm an honorary member, right?"

"If not, she'll figure it out pretty quickly."

I ordered another round of drinks from the bartender. "The guys will be sorry she left. They were enjoying the view."

He arched an eyebrow. "Really? How can they check out another woman when they're sitting in clear view of you?"

"That's your ale talking." I was grateful to have to peer into my purse for money because I could feel the heat permeating my cheeks.

"I don't need four pints to tell you how amazing you look in that dress." He slapped his head. "Gods, I shouldn't have said that. That really is four pints of ale talking."

"Why don't you join us? I'm sure they won't mind. Jayce and Beau have been talking about how much they miss you and Wyatt."

He perked up. "Really?"

"I know a lot of time has passed, but maybe you should think about getting reacquainted."

"Thanks, Rose. I think I've had enough to drink tonight, but that's good to know." He slid off the stool and tossed money on the counter.

I stood still for a moment, watching him swagger out of the bar. He really did look amazing in those jeans.

I took the tray of drinks off the counter and carried it to the booth.

Beau whistled. "Man, I didn't realize you had a thing going with Granger."

I returned to my seat. "I don't."

Beau snorted. "Yeah, right. You were looking at each other the way Jayce here eyes a steak when he's famished."

"We're friends," I said firmly.

"Yeah, I've had friends like that," Jayce said.

"Amanda, Mae, Ruby, Charlotte." Leo laughed. "Need I go on?"

I sipped my ale and listened to the werewolves ribbing each other. I was glad I'd agreed to come. It was the kind of entertaining distraction I needed tonight.

By the time I finished my drink, I was ready for bed. I'd

left my car at coven headquarters, so I called a cab. As we approached Rose Cottage, I was surprised to see my car in the driveway. I retrieved a note tucked under the windshield wiper.

Thought I'd make your morning a little easier tomorrow. - Granger

Maybe it was the result of too much ale, but I started to cry. I slipped the note into my purse and went inside.

CHAPTER SIXTEEN

Are you sure this should be your next step? Raoul asked.

The raccoon and I stood on the sidewalk on Seers Row.

"I've hit a dead end in the case," I explained. "I said I'd leave no stone unturned."

And that means we need a psychic?

"Veronica's not just a psychic, Raoul. She's the Voice of the Gods. Maybe the gods are ready to tell us who killed Roy Nash." It wasn't my usual method, but I was determined to solve this murder. I didn't want to be a failure in every aspect of my life.

Raoul pointed his paw. *Maybe we should consider that one.*

I turned to see a new sign on the building adjacent to Veronica's that read *Seraphina: Louder Voice of the Gods.*

"Well, this is an interesting development," I said.

Which one do we want? Raoul asked. *I feel persuaded by her use of 'Louder.'*

"I don't know that my eardrums could take a decibel louder than Veronica." The psychic had a tendency to screech that I was willing to overlook in favor of her accurate predictions.

Raoul wandered closer to the new shop and pressed his nose against the glass. *I think we should check out the new one. Support a new local business.*

"Why? What do you see?"

Cookies.

"Fair enough." I hurried to enter the other shop, not wanting Veronica to catch a glimpse of me. I didn't need her shrieking 'traitor' until my ears bled.

The ambience of Seraphina's shop was remarkably different from Veronica's. There were white flowers in vases and pots scattered throughout the room. A white West Highland terrier slept on a dog bed that looked like it was made out of marshmallow.

"Welcome," a soothing voice said. "I'm Seraphina."

I smiled at the blonde dressed in a flowing white dress. She had the kind of perfect teeth that only showed up on celebrities or posters in the orthodontist's office.

"I thought you were supposed to be loud," I said.

She flashed a dazzling smile that forced me to squint. "That's only for marketing purposes. It's my connection to the gods that's strong, but Stronger Connection to the Gods doesn't quite have the same ring to it."

Raoul gaped at her with his mouth hanging open until I finally gave him a gentle kick.

"What brings you in today?" she asked.

"I need some guidance," I said.

She gestured to the nearby table covered in a sumptuous white cloth. "Join me, won't you? There are cookies if you're hungry."

Don't mind if I do. Raoul scurried over to the plate. *White chocolate chip. Score!* He stuffed a cookie into his mouth and immediately spat it out again.

"Raoul!"

Macadamia nuts! He started to choke and clutched his neck.

I rushed over. "Are you allergic?"

He looked at me askance. *No, but I hate them.*

I turned to look at Seraphina. "I'm so sorry. I'll clean this up."

"Never mind that. I sense you have more important matters to attend to. I'll deal with it later."

Well, she wasn't wrong about that.

I joined her at the table and tried to get settled. "You don't use a scrying glass?"

She scrunched her nose. "Dear me, no. I find them banal and pedestrian."

I wondered how Veronica would respond to that. Not well, I imagined.

"What do you use then?" I asked, genuinely curious.

She stretched both hands across the table. "Your energy."

Simple enough. I placed my hands in hers.

Ooh, I like where this is going, Raoul said.

I kept my attention on Seraphina. "Do I close my eyes?"

"Yes, that usually works best. I'd like you to picture your first question." Her voice was soothing and encouraging.

I envisioned the picture of Roy Nash from the file—not the one from the crime scene, of course.

"Your energy is delicious," Seraphina said.

That was an odd choice of words. Then again, the yogis in town were always calling stretches 'yummy,' so who was I to judge?

"I'm a descendant of the One True Witch," I said. I didn't bother to mention the recent influx of my ancestor Ivy's power. That tidbit seemed unnecessary.

"That explains the surge of power I feel." She sounded more excited than I expected. Veronica didn't seem to notice or care about any of that.

"I'm picturing the reason I'm here," I said. I kept my eyes squeezed shut.

"I sense you're trying to help someone, but the path has been challenging."

"Yes, that's right. I've reached a dead end and I'd like to know whether I'll have a breakthrough soon." Or a breakdown. Either one was possible.

When Seraphina didn't respond, I peeked one eye open to look at her and my heart skipped a beat. Her shining, angelic face had morphed into a hideous green one. Snakes hissed from her head and a forked tongue slid from between blood-red lips.

My heart pounded and I grabbed Raoul's fur. *Sweet baby Medusa.*

The raccoon shook me off. *What's wrong with you?*

You didn't see that? How could he have missed it?

Seraphina gave me a pleasant smile. "Is something wrong, Miss Rose?"

"No, nothing," I said quickly. I didn't want Hideous Snake Lady to know I was on to her.

"Why don't we try again?" she offered. "I seem to have lost the connection."

I would rather have endured dinner-for-two with Aunt Hyacinth, but I acquiesced. I had no clue what I was dealing with and didn't want to provoke her.

Seraphina wiggled her fingers and I clasped her hand, trying my best not to cringe as my skin touched hers. At least she didn't feel scaly.

"Yes, that's better," she said. "You'd like to know whether you'll find what you seek."

I had a hard time conjuring any more images. The one of Seraphina's face seemed to push everything else out of the way. I released her hands and shot to my feet.

"You know what? I think I'm good."

Seraphina cocked her head. "You seem agitated."

"No, not at all. I just remembered that my daughter has music lessons." I shoved Raoul toward the door. "We'll try again another time."

I haven't seen you move this fast since the All-You-Can-Eat buffet at the seafood restaurant.

We slipped into the neighboring parlor trying not to appear guilty. Jericho, Veronica's assistant, stood in front of us with his arms folded.

"You were next door, weren't you?" he demanded.

I licked my lips. "Maybe."

"What were you doing in there? Don't you know that place is verboten?" Jericho hissed.

"We weren't paying attention and wandered in by accident," I lied.

"I'm glad my liege didn't see you." He looked traumatized by the mere possibility. "I couldn't handle another tirade today."

"Not been a good day, huh?"

"She accidentally picked up a bottle of correction fluid instead of polish and now her nails are the color of milk." He paused for dramatic effect. "She hates milk."

Veronica emerged from the back room and broke into a broad smile at the sight of me. "Emma, you're back!"

"Ember," I corrected her.

"Right, of course." She flicked a dismissive finger. "Ember Rosenberg. The Voice of the Gods never forgets."

"Rose," I said. "Ember Rose."

She ignored me and gestured to her table. "Join me. What message from the gods do you seek today?"

"I'm stuck on a matter and can use help in the form of information."

I sat across from her.

"Jericho," she shrieked. "I need water, preferably

sparkling." She smiled at me. "The voice of the gods is so much clearer when bubbles are involved."

"Yes, fairest one of all." Jericho hobbled over with a bottle of sparkling water and twisted off the lid, careful not to let the bottle explode.

Veronica tipped back the bottle and chugged. She drained it dry and handed the empty bottle to her assistant.

"That's better," she said. "Scrying is thirsty work." She stared at the orb. "You've come looking for answers from the gods, have you?"

"Yes, I've been looking into…"

Veronica shushed me. "I'm getting something." She wrapped her arms around the scrying glass and hugged it to her chest. "You're on the right track, Emily."

"Ember." I paused. "How can I be on the right track? I don't have any more leads."

Veronica rubbed her palms against the scrying glass. "The gods want you to know that appearances can be deceiving."

"Can the gods be a little more specific?" I asked.

Veronica pressed her lips against the scrying glass. If I saw any tongue, I was out of here. I'd had enough of strange encounters with psychics for one day.

"The death was an accident," Veronica said.

I reeled back. An accident? But how? "Do you see what happened?"

Veronica snapped her fingers and Jericho hurried over with another bottle of water. If she didn't slow down, she'd need a bathroom break before we'd finished.

"I see tears," Veronica said. "Followed by immense grief and sorrow."

"Well, yes. That's what happens when someone dies. Can you see what killed the werewolf?"

Veronica snapped out of her trance and looked at me. "Werewolf? I'm not talking about the death of a werewolf."

I frowned. "Then what are you talking about?"

She took a long sip from the bottle before answering. "I'm talking about the death of a cat."

I leaned back against the chair, feeling confused. "A cat?"

Raoul's voice cut through my thoughts. *Jingles.*

"Are you talking about Jingles?" I asked.

"That's right. Jingles." Veronica glanced up from the scrying glass, her eyes wide. "Jingles is dead because her witch accidentally killed her."

Well, I guess that's the end of that. Time to move on to the next one. Raoul dusted off his paws as we exited Veronica's shop.

"What makes you say that?"

He squinted at me with his beady eyes. *You did hear the lady, right?*

"She's pretty loud. Kind of hard not to."

Violet killed her familiar. We can't approve her for Arnold Palmer.

"It was an accident," I said. I opened the car door for Raoul and then went around to the driver's side.

What don't you know? You'd rather wait and see if she kills Arnold Palmer and then decide it's not a good idea?

I started the car and looked at him. "Violet has been punishing herself ever since his death."

No kidding. The cottage and gardens have been punished too.

"I don't think we should rule her out."

Raoul slapped his paws over his eyes. *Why do you have to see everything as complicated?*

I checked my mirrors and pulled onto the road. "You saw Violet. That witch is depressed."

Yeah, she's depressed because she murdered Jingles.

"Accidentally and she clearly blames herself."

As she should. I'm a little concerned how blasé you're being about the accidental death of a familiar.

"She doesn't even want to replace Jingles. She's afraid."

Because she feels guilty. She worries she'll do it again, which is why we can't subject Arnold Palmer to her.

I shook my head. "You're being too hard on Violet."

I'm not sure you're in the best mental place to make that determination.

I glared at him. "My own situation is *not* coloring my judgment."

Raoul peered out the window. *Where are we going? This isn't the way home.*

"No, we're going to Violet's."

Raoul's head swiveled toward me. *What? No way. I'm not in the mood to be roasted on a spit.*

"Relax. I can take down Violet with one hand tied behind my back if necessary."

Are you sure about that? She made a whole pot of tea with one hand and you can't even operate the microwave with one finger.

"I'm a pro now. I've even learned to use the melting feature!"

I sped along the coastal road, paying such close attention to my conversation with Raoul that I failed to notice the red lights flashing until they were directly behind me.

"What does Bolan want?" I muttered. I pulled off the road and rolled down my window.

I doubt he wants to congratulate you on your excellent driving.

"Ma'am, do you know how fast you were driving?"

Ma'am? I narrowed my eyes at the deputy outside my door. "Hello, Deputy Pitt."

Va-va-voom, Raoul said. I half expected his eyes to spring out of his head and uncoil like in the cartoons.

Keep your thoughts to yourself, I warned.

"Oh, Ember, right? I'm so sorry to have to pull you over, but you were speeding."

"Was I? I thought I was sticking to the limit pretty closely."

Deputy Pitt offered an apologetic smile. "No, I'm sorry, but you were going six miles over the limit. I clocked you."

Maybe you should clock her.

I shushed Raoul in my head. "Well, I'm sorry, Deputy Pitt. It won't happen again."

Until the next time it happens.

She took out her notepad and filled in the information on the ticket before handing it to me. "The fine isn't too bad. I've seen a lot higher ones."

"I'm sure my unemployment check will cover it," I said.

The werewolf winced. "Gods, that's right. Granger mentioned you got fired."

Granger? Raoul echoed. *That's not very professional.*

I set the ticket in the cupholder between the seats. "It's fine. I can afford it."

"Maybe next time, try to keep an eye on the speedometer," Deputy Pitt said. "It doesn't pay to speed."

"Sure thing. You shouldn't apologize, by the way," I said.

She leaned closer to the window. "I beg your pardon?"

"For pulling someone over. A man would never apologize for doing his job. Neither should you."

Deputy Pitt didn't seem to know how to respond. "Oh, okay. Thanks for the tip."

"Don't mention it." I started the car.

You let her give you a ticket, Raoul said. *You didn't even give her any attitude. Are you feeling okay?*

I shrugged. "I didn't want to give her a hard time." Well, I did, but I resisted the urge.

Because you were, in fact, speeding?

"Because she's going to have to deal with a lot worse than me in that job. There's no reason to make it any harder for her."

Raoul's gaze lingered on me.

"What?" I asked.

The raccoon slipped down into his seat. *Nothing.*

I rejoined the road and continued to the far end of town.

Do we have to listen to Springsteen? he complained. *There are other musicians in the world, you know.*

"Why? Who would you rather listen to?"

I'm partial to smooth jazz.

I barked a laugh. "I would rather be tortured on the rack than listen to anything with the word 'jazz' in it."

You like jazz hands.

"That's different. Jazz hands are fun." I lifted my hands off the wheel to demonstrate. "Listening to jazz is another experience entirely."

I turned onto the dirt road that would take us deeper into the woods.

"I should've ridden my broomstick. It would've been easier."

I don't know about that. You would've hit about thirty branches on the landing.

"My landing skills are excellent."

He shrugged. *I've seen better.*

Violet's cottage looked exactly the same as the last time we were here. Overgrown garden. Rusted door. Faded shutters. She clearly hadn't taken any steps to remedy the poor condition of her home since our visit.

Be careful. She might greet us with a shotgun this time.

"She's a witch. If anything, she'll use magic."

You're not making me feel any better.

We made our way to the door and I knocked once.

That's it?

"What's it?"

You tapped the door like you were congratulating it on a job well done.

"It stayed on its hinges, didn't it?"

"Come in, trespassers," Violet called.

I opened the door to the cottage and saw Violet in her usual spot in the rocking chair with an open book on her lap.

"You two again?" the witch asked. "I would've thought I put you off coming back here."

"The tea wasn't *that* bad," I said, smiling.

"What do you want?" she asked, her tone apprehensive.

I moved further into the room with Raoul clinging to my pant leg. "The thing is, Violet, I know another reclusive witch in Starry Hollow. Her name is Artemis Haverford."

Violet closed the book on her lap. "Yes, I've heard of her."

"Artemis rarely leaves Haverford House. She's happy at home with her ghostly manservant, Jefferson." I waved a dismissive hand. "That's a long story. Anyway, the point is that Artemis isn't reclusive because she's awful and unpleasant. In fact, it's quite the opposite."

"And what does that have to do with me?"

I clasped my hands in front of me. "I don't think you're awful or unpleasant either, no matter what you'd have us believe."

Violet scowled. "Well, you're wrong about that. I'm so awful that I killed my own familiar. Did you know that?"

"It was an accident, though, wasn't it?" I asked softly. "A horrible accident and you've been torturing yourself over it ever since."

Violet's eyes widened slightly. "I'm doing no such thing. I'm a cranky, horrible witch. I live out here alone because I hate being around others. They make me want to cast a spell and put them all to sleep so I don't have to listen to them blather on about their dull, insignificant lives."

Raoul leaned closer. *She sounds convincing to me. We should go.*

I inched closer to Violet. "I don't believe you. I think the death of Jingles sent you over the edge and you haven't been able to ask for help because you think you don't deserve it."

I thought of Alec. The vampire's resistance to opening up and letting himself be vulnerable started here—in the same kind of mental place that Violet was currently trapped in. I refused to let the same thing happen to the young witch. She'd end up alone for the rest of her life and the world would be deprived of what she had to offer.

"You're absolutely right. I don't deserve it." Violet pulled the blanket higher and clutched it against her chest. "You should go before I turn you both into toads. I'm very adept at that one. I practice all the time."

"Violet, tell us what really happened to Jingles," I urged gently. "We know it was an accident. Why not tell us the truth?"

Violet turned to gaze out the window. "I was working on a complicated spell in the garden. Jingles usually wore a tiny bell on a collar around her neck. That's how she got her name."

Don't ever do that to me, Raoul said. *I'm not a cow.*

"I'd taken off her collar the night before to wash it and forgotten. She'd tangled with a skunk earlier that day and I couldn't get the smell out." Violet drew her knees to her chest. "I didn't realize she was there. She was hidden behind the hydrangeas and the spell went wrong."

"You didn't sense her presence?"

Sniffing, Violet shook her head. "I was too focused on the spell to notice. I accidentally launched a fireball. It burned straight through the hydrangeas and hit Jingles. There was nothing I could do. I took her to the healer's, but it was too late."

I couldn't imagine how difficult that must've been for Violet. "I'm so sorry, Violet."

She looked at me with tears glistening in her eyes. "Now do you understand why I can't have another familiar?"

"It was an accident," I countered. "A horrible, tragic accident."

"One accident is enough, don't you think? Especially one that took the life of an innocent cat."

"Is that why you retreated from coven life? Stopped volunteering at gardening events?" I asked.

Violet blew out a breath. "There was no joy in it, not that I deserved to feel anything good."

"You can't punish yourself forever," I said.

Violet jerked her head toward me. "Can't I? I think I've gotten pretty good at it."

"You have your whole life ahead of you. Jingles wouldn't want you to give up at the start."

"No, Jingles would want me to burn in hell where I belong." Violet leaned her back against the chair and rocked. "I'm surprised a bolt of lightning hasn't claimed me yet."

I take it all back, Raoul said. *She's hurting, not horrible.*

You're finally seeing it my way, huh?

She needs someone, Raoul said.

I agreed. And that someone was Arnold Palmer.

CHAPTER SEVENTEEN

I PARKED in the semi-circular driveway of Haverford House and the first thing I noticed was a new bench that featured two skeletons. One held up a pair of binoculars to its empty eye sockets and the other one held a copy of *War and Peace* in its bony fingers.

"Um, Mom?" Marley exited the car and went over to inspect the display. "Is she decorating for Halloween or something?"

"I doubt it since every day is Halloween here."

I rang the bell and waited for Jefferson to answer. The door creaked open and Marley and I entered the foyer and walked straight through to the front parlor room where Artemis awaited us.

"What a pleasant surprise," the elderly witch said. "My two favorite witches." Instead of her usual white dress that made her look like she'd been jilted at the altar a century ago, today she wore a tasteful dress in pale pink. It was a nice change.

"Marley and I wanted to check in and see how you're doing," I said. My visit to Violet reminded me how important it was to stay connected with paranormals like Artemis, who spent most of their time alone.

"What I really want to know is why you have skeletons out front," Marley interjected.

"It's an art installation," Artemis said. "A marvelous piece called Patience by a local artist named Weaver. A very talented young gargoyle."

"And you keep it there forever?" I asked.

"Oh, no," Artemis said. "It travels. The piece will be displayed here for a few weeks before moving on to another showcase."

Well, at least we wouldn't be stuck looking at it every time we came to visit.

"Tea, please, Jefferson," Artemis said.

A blast of air streaked past me as the ghostly manservant made his way to the kitchen and I shivered in response.

"Please sit down," she instructed us. "I feel anxious when others are standing while I'm sitting."

Marley and I sat next to each other on the loveseat.

"I am so very sorry about everything you're going through," Artemis said.

I smiled. "I wasn't sure whether you'd heard the news."

Artemis clucked her tongue. "Hyacinth is a fool and Alec even more so. I'd feel sorry for them if they weren't so misguided in their actions."

"I'm not worried about either one of them," I said.

"I'm more concerned for the two of you." The elderly witch fidgeted with the hem of her sleeve. "To have found your missing family only to have them turn their backs on you..." Her expression grew pained. "It can't be easy for you."

"Only Aunt Hyacinth has turned her back on me. My cousins are being as supportive as they can be."

"But everyone fears Hyacinth in this town. The road ahead will undoubtedly be bumpy."

I forced a smile. "Then it's a good thing I have extra cushioning on my backside."

"I was having trouble at school, but that's taken care of," Marley said.

I swiveled to look at her. "It is? Since when?"

Marley smiled. "Since I cast a spell on them."

Artemis leaned forward with interest. "What kind of spell did you use, dear?"

"An opposite spell," Marley said. "Every time they tried to do or say anything mean, the opposite happened. If they tried to ruin my homework, they ruined their own homework. If they tried to say something mean to me in front of other kids, they ended up saying something really nice instead." She beamed. "It worked like a charm—because it was one."

"And you think this will be the end of it?" I asked.

"I think they got a dose of their own medicine and I feel pretty confident that it tasted bad enough to heal them, so to speak," Marley said.

I leaned over and hugged her. "Good for you. I'm so proud of you."

"I told you I could handle it," she whispered and I heard the note of pride in her voice. This new confident Marley was a breath of fresh air.

"And what will you do for work, Ember?" Artemis asked.

"I've been job hunting. Had a few interviews but nothing has panned out yet." Although I'd been thinking about what Mr. Mayhew had said about taking stock of my skills.

Artemis licked her chapped lips. "Shall I take a peek at your future?"

"Not today, thanks."

A tray with a teapot and three cups floated to rest on the console table. An unseen hand filled three cups from the pot and delivered them to us.

"And how are you taking it, Marley?" Artemis asked.

"I think Aunt Hyacinth is being unreasonable but she'll come to her senses eventually."

Artemis gave me a knowing look. "But you don't?"

"I know Aunt Hyacinth. She's been after Ivy's magic for years. There's no way she'll be able to stand having it within reach yet not hers."

"Would you mind if I have a look at the herb garden?" Marley asked.

"I'd be disappointed if you didn't," Artemis said.

Marley raced from the parlor room to the kitchen where the side door was located.

"Are you quite sure you won't give the magic to her?" Artemis asked.

I gave my head an adamant shake. "Absolutely not."

Artemis brought a shaky cup to her lips and sipped. "But why keep it when it's caused so much trouble? It's not as though you crave more power."

I clasped my hands in my lap. "No, but that doesn't mean I think my aunt should have it. Besides, I can't explain it, but I feel a connection to Ivy and I think she'd be disappointed if I passed her power to Aunt Hyacinth. She went to a lot of trouble to hide it away and she seems content for me to have it."

"But that was to keep the coven from stripping her of it rather to keep it out of the wrong hands, wasn't it?" Artemis pressed.

I picked up a teacup. "Regardless, nothing good comes from too much concentrated power in one place. Aunt Hyacinth already has more than her fair share. Like you said, everyone's afraid of her. How can the answer to that be to give her more power?"

Clementine strode into the parlor room and jumped onto the witch's lap. Artemis absently stroked her back. "You make a strong argument, Ember. I only wish your actions didn't result in a target on your back."

"Oh, I'm pretty sure the target is right here." I thumped my chest. "My aunt has made no bones about her dismay."

Marley entered the room carrying a green pot with a thriving plant. "Do you mind if I take this one home with us to add to the garden, Artemis?"

"Of course not," the elderly witch replied. "My garden is your garden, my dear."

"Thank you." Marley held up the plant for inspection. "This will make a great addition to the team."

Artemis smiled. "The team. I love the way your mind works, Marley." She reached over and patted my leg. "Whatever happens with your aunt, you're doing something very right, Ember."

I felt a rush of pride. My daughter was, indeed, shaping up to be a remarkable young woman. She was destined to win over the world with her intelligence and compassion rather than her power. I might not be suitable for employment or a romantic relationship, but I seemed to be suitable as a mother and that counted for a lot.

"There's nothing so powerful as a mother's love," Artemis mused. "Perhaps Hyacinth would do well to remember that and leave well enough alone."

"Do you regret not having children of your own?" I asked.

She kissed the top of Clementine's head. "No. I've been quite content with my life, though I know it doesn't appeal to everyone. There are other kinds of love, each with its own potency." She sighed softly. "The wonderful thing about motherhood, of course, is knowing that your unconditional love is returned. Other types of love aren't so reliable, sadly."

"There are no guarantees," I said. I'd seen enough episodes of 60 Minutes to know the dark side of unrequited love. When what was once passion morphed into hatred and jealousy and ended in—

Murder.

I nearly dropped my cup as the realization swept over me. I remembered the look on Betty Hickok's face when she talked about Roy Nash. The amount of time the couples spent together and the bickering between Barnaby and Betty. The sheriff had investigated Barnaby but not Betty. The affair may have been imagined, but that didn't mean Barnaby was wrong about his wife's feelings for Roy.

I set down the cup and grabbed my purse from the floor. "I'm so sorry, Artemis. I need to go. Would you mind keeping Marley here with you for a bit?"

Marley shot me a quizzical glance. "What is it, Mom?"

"Hopefully nothing." I smiled to put her at ease. "I'll be back before dinner. I promise."

"No rush, my dear. Marley is welcome to stay here as long as you like." Artemis rubbed the underside of the cat's neck. "Isn't that right, Clementine?"

The mangy cat meowed her answer.

"Thank you so much. I really appreciate it." I hurried from the house before I could blurt out the real reason for my hasty exit. I didn't want to worry them. If I was right, then Granger Nash would finally be able to give up the ghost—in this case, not a hunky manservant, but his father, the werewolf that Betty Hickok was hopelessly in love with.

So hopeless, in fact, that she killed him.

It seemed that I'd arrived at Betty's condo in the nick of time. The door was propped open and the interior was mostly empty. The boxes were gone and I found Betty alone with a wicker basket full of cleaning supplies. She wore a bandana over her head and an Arizona Cardinals T-shirt with matching sweatpants.

"Hello, Betty."

She splayed a hand across her chest, appearing surprised. "Ember, you startled me. I didn't expect to see you again."

I nodded to the basket. "Getting ready for the final walk-through?"

"It isn't until next week, but I'll be leaving before then, so I want to get it done." She frowned. "What are you doing here?"

Stopping you from fleeing the jurisdiction before your arrest. "I've been working on the Nash case and I put together a missing piece of the puzzle. I thought I might run it by you for confirmation."

Betty blinked rapidly. "Run it by me? Why would I be the best one to ask about it?"

"Because you're the one who was in love with him."

Slowly, she set the wicker basket on the floor. "I don't know what you mean. The affair was only in Barnaby's head because of the anniversary gift. You know all that."

"No, not just because of that," I said. "Because he sensed something more. Your husband sensed that you had feelings for Roy Nash and he was right."

Betty laughed awkwardly. "Don't be absurd. We were very close, but only as couples who spent a lot of time together. There was no affair."

"I believe you that there was no affair, but that doesn't mean you weren't in love with him."

Betty glanced away, but the two bright pink spots that formed on her cheeks told me what I needed to know.

"And you mistakenly believed he was in love with you, too," I continued.

When Betty finally spoke, her voice was low and thick with emotion. "I misunderstood the signals. We spent so much time together, the four of us. My boys ran wild and it put a strain on the marriage. I reached a point when I knew I didn't love my husband anymore and I thought Roy was in the same boat."

"What happened? You floated the idea of running away together and he shot you down?"

"It was so humiliating." She lowered her gaze to the floor, seeming to relive the moment. "I've never felt so stupid in my whole life."

"And then what? The rejection was too much for you? You got angry and killed him?"

Betty's head swiveled back toward me. "Killed him? No. Never." Pain radiated from her. "By the gods, his death nearly broke me." She wiped a tear from her face with the back of her hand. "I was such a mess. And then Barnaby was a suspect…It was the worst time of our lives."

"And yet you stayed married to Barnaby," I said.

Her eyes sparkled with grief. "What else could I do? There was no Roy to dream of anymore. I decided it was best for the boys if we stayed together. They sensed the discord. In hindsight, I think it's half the reason they were acting up."

That fit with what Beau and Arthur had told me. "What about Marianne? She was supposed to be your friend."

Betty pressed the pads of her fingers against her cheeks, as though detecting the warmth that had gathered there. "The truth is I didn't care very much for her. I only tolerated her because I wanted to spend time with Roy. After he died, I saw no real reason to stay friends anymore."

Then it wasn't the fact that she'd murdered Roy that destroyed the friendship; it was the fact Betty hadn't liked Marianne in the first place. Neither scenario painted Betty in the best light.

"I've thought about it a lot over the years," Betty said, "and I'm not proud of my behavior. In fact, I'm downright ashamed, but I had nothing to do with Roy's death. I remember watching my boys play and thinking how fortunate they were to still have their father. I felt terrible for the Nash boys, losing their father so young. It's no wonder Wyatt never got his act together. My boys would've been the same if our family had fallen apart."

"Did you tell Barnaby you were in love with Roy?" I asked.

Betty fished a tissue from her pocket and dabbed at the corners of her eyes. "Not in so many words. Over time, things calmed down between us and the boys mellowed. I wouldn't say the marriage ever fully recovered, but it served its purpose."

"Then you weren't the one who lured Roy into the woods that day," I said, more of a statement than a question.

"No, I was home making dinner. I remember it well because I burned the lasagna waiting for the boys to come home. I was furious—until I heard the news about Roy, of course. Then I was catatonic."

"Beau had been with Arthur Rutledge."

She cocked her head at me. "That's right. And Jayce was gods-knew-where. Came home a mess and I sent him straight to the shower. He was as bad as Beau at the time, although he wasn't willing to accept help. I think he took the role of older son too seriously sometimes."

My head started to spin. I was so wrapped up in my thoughts that I failed to hear the sound of footsteps behind me.

"Here's Jayce now," Betty said. "You can ask him about it yourself."

Jayce stood in the doorway with a toolbox in one hand and a wrench in the other. "What's going on?"

"I should ask you the same thing," I said, slowly turning to face him. My pulse quickened, wondering whether he'd heard any of our conversation.

He glanced at the wrench in his hand. "Mom asked me to fix the toilet before she hands in the keys so the landlord doesn't keep part of the security deposit."

I turned back to Betty and felt a hard thwack across the back of my head.

Apparently, Jayce had heard enough.

CHAPTER EIGHTEEN

WHEN I FINALLY REGAINED CONSCIOUSNESS, my wrists were bound behind me and my torso was strapped to the tank of a toilet with duct tape. The back of my head throbbed, but I couldn't move my hands to rub it.

"She's awake."

Betty came into focus in the doorway of the bathroom. Jayce loomed behind her, looking agitated.

"Seriously?" I said. "A toilet? You couldn't find somewhere more unsanitary to kill me?"

"I didn't have much to work with in an empty condo, did I?" Jayce said.

"I promise you it's clean," Betty said. "I had the whole place scrubbed after the boxes were cleared out."

"Yes, but now you won't get your full security deposit back," I said. "Jayce can't fix the toilet with a dead body on it."

Jayce laughed. "Joke's on you. I fixed it before I strapped you to it. I knocked out two problems with one wrench." He inclined his head to the toolbox and wrench on the floor between the sink and the toilet.

"So what's your plan, Jayce?" I asked. I saw no reason to

play dumb at this point. He'd shown his hand by attacking me and the more I could stall for time, the better chance I had of freeing myself from the tape.

"My plan is for my secret to die with you," he said. "This place will be empty for at least a week. Nobody will think to look for you here."

He was right. I hadn't told anyone where I was going. At least Marley was safe with Artemis, although she'd worry if I wasn't back soon.

"Except your secret won't die with me," I said. "Now your mom knows the truth. Do you plan to kill her, too?"

Jayce gave his mother a quick squeeze and she stiffened at his touch. "My mom will lock it in the vault, along with her other secret about Roy."

I shot a pleading glance at Betty. "Please don't let him do this," I said, continuing to pick at the tape behind my back. If I could free my torso, I could worry about my wrists later.

She looked between us, clearly struggling with a decision. "He's my son, Ember."

"Your son is a killer," I said. "He murdered Roy, the werewolf you loved."

Betty removed her bandana from her head and twisted it with her hands. "I lost Roy, and then Barnaby. I can't afford to lose Jayce, too."

"I have a daughter, Marley," I said. "Her father's already dead. If something happens to me, she'll be an orphan. Is that what you want? Does my innocent child deserve to be left without a family?"

Jayce stepped between us and faced his mother. "Mom, why don't you leave? It's best not to have any witnesses."

"That's right. You're an expert," I said. "You lured Roy Nash into the woods to avoid that very problem, didn't you?"

Jayce had the nerve to smirk. "I pretended to be injured.

He couldn't resist playing the role of savior. Just like he tried to save my mom from her crappy marriage."

"Just like you killed him to save your family," I said. "Ironic, isn't it?"

"Roy was going to ruin our lives," Jayce growled. "He was going to run away with my mom and destroy two families."

"No, Jayce," Betty said quietly. "Roy had no intention of leaving Marianne."

Jayce gaped at her. "He wanted to keep you as his mistress? That's even worse."

"No." She kept her gaze fixed on her son. "There was no affair, Jayce. Roy didn't love me. In fact, he never so much as kissed me. I was so unhappy in my marriage that I misread the signals. If anyone's to blame, it's me."

Jayce's brow furrowed. "No, you're lying."

"Why would she lie?" I interjected.

Jayce's face reddened. "Mom, I want you to go. *Now*. And don't come back."

Betty stifled a cry as she fled the bathroom. Oddly enough, I didn't blame her. Jayce was her child. Of course, she would choose him over me.

The werewolf turned his attention back to me. "I wish you hadn't pieced it together and we could all go on with our lives."

"But you haven't gone on with your life, Jayce," I said. "You've wanted to, but you haven't managed it, have you?"

He scowled. "Of course I have."

"That's why you drifted apart from Wyatt and Granger. You felt guilty, knowing what you'd done to their father."

"Roy got what he deserved," he snarled.

"What you *thought* he deserved." I paused. "But you knew it was wrong, just like you know this is wrong."

"I kept my family intact," Jayce said. "I regret nothing."

"And you sacrificed the Nash family in order to make that happen."

"It's Roy's fault. If he hadn't led my mom on, made her believe he loved her…" He trailed off.

"He didn't make her believe anything. Your mother was unhappy and gravitated to the nearest port in a storm. Roy was a friendly, standup guy. It's no wonder she pinned all her hopes and dreams on him, but that's all it was, Jayce. A fantasy she constructed for herself to cope with her misery."

"Enough!" Jayce raised a hand and smacked me across the face. Pain bloomed and I closed my eyes in an effort not to cry.

"How do you expect to get away with this? Once they find me, how long do you think it will take for the murder to be traced back to you? I'm in your mother's condo, Jayce."

"But my mother will be in Arizona. She wasn't even in Starry Hollow when you died. You came looking for her and didn't find her. While you were nosing around here, you hurt yourself and couldn't make your way out."

"There are way too many holes in that story," I said. "What about my phone? My magic?"

"You can't do magic in here," he said. "One of the annoying things about this condo. None of us could shift until we went outside."

"How do you plan to kill me so it looks like an accident? I'm strapped to a freakin' toilet, Jayce."

Jayce's eyes flickered with uncertainty as he seemed to contemplate the loose ends.

"Not as easy as snapping a neck in the woods, is it?" I pressed. "This one takes more thought and planning."

Jayce cracked his knuckles. "An intruder found you here and mistook you for the owner. Strangled you and fled."

"You know that Granger and I have a special relationship.

You said so yourself at the Wishing Well. Do you really think he's going to let this case go unsolved?"

"He never discovered who killed his daddy," Jayce said, appearing smug. "Don't see why this one will be any different."

"Because he was only a kid when his father died," I said. "He's the sheriff now. There's also the issue of my aunt."

He frowned. "Your aunt."

"Hyacinth Rose-Muldoon." Just because we were on the outs didn't mean she wouldn't bring the weight of House Rose down upon my killer's head. She would have a reputation to protect.

Jayce flinched. "That's right. I forgot she's your aunt. She's pretty powerful."

"There's something else you apparently don't know."

He folded his arms. "What's that?"

I lifted my chin. "I'm powerful, too."

Jayce clucked his tongue. "I'm sure you are, sweetheart, but like I said, there's no magic in this building. Tough break, witch."

"Funny, I was just about to say the same to you."

I freed my body from the toilet and launched myself at Jayce headfirst. I knew I wasn't strong enough to take him in a physical fight and my wrists were still bound behind my back, but he was blocking the only exit. If I expected to get past him, I had to move him out of the way somehow.

Jayce staggered backward, surprised by the sudden move. Before I could get away, He punched me in the stomach and I flew back through the shower curtain and into the bathtub. I gasped for air and sank into the tub.

It was then that I glimpsed the window behind me. I'd bet Aunt Hyacinth's fortune there was a fire escape out there, which meant there was another way out after all. Jayce would expect me to run toward him, not away from him. I scrambled to my feet and bolted for the window.

"Where do you think…?" He must've realized where I was headed and chased after me.

I climbed onto the ledge of the tub and turned, pushing up the unlocked window with my bound hands. I managed to get one leg over the sill before Jayce grabbed me. He tried to pull me back into the bathroom, but I slipped from his grasp and landed on the fire escape with the grace of a drunken toddler and prepared to climb down seven flights of steps. Until I realized I had a better option.

I was no longer inside of the condo.

Relegare, I said. The same spell I'd used to remove the floorboard in the sheriff's office would also work to remove the duct tape.

Jayce growled. "Come back here, you…"

"*Obliviscatur*," I said, throwing out my hands.

Jayce blinked and shook his head. "Who are you? What's going on?"

Hopefully, Jayce would stay confused long enough for me to call Sheriff Nash. I reached into my pocket for my phone and realized it was in my purse still inside the condo.

Crap on a cracker.

Unfortunately, Jayce recovered his senses more quickly than I anticipated.

"You don't seem that powerful to me," he said. "Your magic must have gotten diluted with each new generation."

I resisted the urge to tell him about Ivy. He'd learn soon enough.

I pulled magical energy from my core and released it. "*Pello!*"

Jayce blew backward out of the bathroom and slammed against the wall in the hallway. I climbed back in through the window and raced to the living room for my purse, scooping up the wrench along the way.

Jayce lumbered into the living room after me and knocked the purse from my hand before I could retrieve the phone. I swung the wrench and felt the crack of metal as it struck his hard jaw.

I didn't wait for his reaction. I immediately hit him again, this time jabbing the end of the wrench into his eye. He howled in pain and clutched his eye.

"You're going to regret that," he snarled.

"Not as much as you're going to regret trying to kill me." I picked up the heavy tool box and smashed the side of his head with it.

The werewolf staggered to the side and collapsed. Blood gushed from the wound.

I grabbed my purse again and searched for my phone. One of these days I was going to be smart and use the front pocket that separated it from the rest of the contents.

As I tapped the screen, the door burst open and the sheriff appeared alongside Raoul.

"Rose, are you okay?" He ran over and gripped me by the shoulders, examining me closely.

"I am now. Can't say the same for Jayce." I looked down at the unconscious figure on the floor.

"Jayce," the sheriff murmured, seemingly confused.

I blew out a quiet breath. "I hate to be the bearer of bad news, but Jayce killed your father and he just tried to kill me to keep me quiet."

The sheriff's expression darkened as he looked at his old friend. "That explains why Betty called me."

I balked. "Betty told you to come here?" I asked. She'd come through after all. That had to be the most difficult phone call she'd ever made.

"Yes," the sheriff said. "She said you might need my help

and gave me the address. When I ran into this guy outside, I knew you were in danger."

Raoul tapped his head. *And I woke up from a nap with a horrible headache. Unfortunately, I know the difference between a hangover and a solid beating.*

I rubbed the back of my head. "Yeah, Jayce is a pretty strong guy." And I had the residual pain to prove it.

"He always has been," the sheriff said grimly. "Even when we were teenagers."

Strong enough to break Roy Nash's neck, apparently, I thought to myself. There was no need to say it out loud. The sheriff knew.

"Jayce lured your dad to the clearing in the woods, knowing it would be empty at that hour. He pretended to be hurt and need help. Your dad must've realized his intentions and tried to shift to get away, but Jayce killed him first."

The sheriff stared at the figure on the floor. "He believed the rumor about the affair."

"He thought your dad was going to break up his family."

Jayce began to stir and the sheriff produced a set of silver handcuffs. "I'll take it from here, Rose," he said grimly.

Wait. What about the drive-thru? Raoul asked.

What are you talking about? I asked.

I thought we could hit the drive-thru lane after this. Order a few tacos to go. Near death experiences make me hungry.

You weren't the one near death, I pointed out.

I'm near you, aren't I?

And that counts?

The raccoon glanced at his rumbling stomach. *Apparently.*

I shook my head. *Somehow I doubt the sheriff was aware of your plan.* I patted my familiar on the head. "Come on, buddy. I'll drive you."

CHAPTER NINETEEN

I AWOKE the next morning to the aroma of coffee and dragged myself downstairs to find a steaming mug on the dining table. It was like an oasis in the desert.

"What's this?" I asked.

Bonkers blinked at me from the scratching post. The front door opened and Marley entered the cottage with PP3 on a leash.

"You took the dog out by yourself?" I asked.

Raoul appeared behind her. *Not entirely.*

"How's your head?" Marley asked. She'd heard the whole terrifying story last night after I'd picked her up from Haverford House.

"Better, thanks."

"You missed Arnold Palmer," Marley said. "He came by earlier to say thank you. He met Violet and they've decided they're a match."

Talk about stealing my thunder, Raoul grumbled. *I was going to tell you that.*

"That's great news," I said. And not remotely a surprise. I

knew in my gut that Violet was the right choice for the pink fairy armadillo. Between the garden and the kitchen, he'd certainly have the kind of work he'd been itching for and Violet needed someone with a tender heart like Arnold Palmer.

Marley unhooked the leash and hung it by the door. "I invited Arnold Palmer and Violet for dinner tonight. I hope you don't mind."

"I think that's a great idea."

She also told him you'd cook, Raoul added. *Still think it's a great idea?*

I looked at Raoul. "I hope one day Arnold Palmer and Violet are as happy as we are."

The raccoon fixed his beady eyes on me. *To me, you're trash.*

That's the nicest compliment you've ever given me.

We misfits have to stick together.

I'm not a misfit, I objected.

He tapped his paw on his cheek. *Let's see. Cast out by your family. Different from the others. A little weird.* He paused. *A lot weird. Yep, I think you qualify.*

"Whatever," I huffed.

There's nothing wrong with being a misfit. We're the best kind of...fits.

That's not a word.

It is now.

"I don't mean to doubt your abilities," Marley began, "but I'm going to suggest you practice before we actually have to feed anyone. We don't want to scare them off."

I grabbed my coffee cup from the table and sauntered into the kitchen. "There's no time like the present. Do we have everything we need?"

Marley ducked into the pantry. "We will in a minute."

What are you making?

I don't know yet. Something that involves chopping onions. I want Arnold Palmer to see that he taught me something useful.

I washed my hands and wiped them on the kitchen towel. "I'm not making any promises about the result. It might taste like garbage."

Raoul kissed his paw. *Perfect.*

PP3 growled and bolted from the kitchen, prompting Marley to peek out the kitchen window.

"Sheriff Nash is here," she said.

I left the kitchen to answer the door. Sure enough, the sheriff stood on the doorstep holding a tray of herbs.

"Hope I didn't come by too early," he said. "I thought you might be sleeping off a headache."

"I took a potion before bed," I said. "Feels like a whole new head."

"Hope not," he said, grinning. "I kind of like the one you have. Anyway, I wanted to bring these for your garden as a thank you. I know it's not enough, but…"

I accepted the tray with gratitude. "You don't need to bring anything. I was happy to help." I scanned the four pots. "What are they?"

He scratched his head. "No idea, but Rick said they'd be good for your magic garden."

Marley rushed over to relieve me of the tray. "These are great. Thank you so much."

"Why don't you take them into the kitchen and give them a little water?" I told her.

"They don't need water yet," Marley said.

I gave her a pointed look. "Then why don't you take them into the kitchen and pretend they need water."

She carried the tray away and disappeared into the kitchen.

The sheriff looked at me with his soulful brown eyes. "I mean it, Rose. My family is forever in your debt."

"I don't want you to be in my debt," I said. "With great power comes great responsibility and all that nonsense."

He gave me a wry grin. "Except you don't think it's nonsense at all."

"No, I guess not."

"I'm sorry I put you in danger."

I laughed. "When am I not in danger? That's like telling a sloth I'm sorry I made you slow."

He chuckled. "Same old Rose."

"Were you expecting someone else?"

He leaned against the doorjamb. "Never."

"I'm sorry about Jayce." I knew how it felt to be betrayed by someone close to you.

"Don't be. I'm just glad to finally know the truth. I'll be sleeping easier from now on thanks to you."

We stood smiling at each other.

"I should probably go," I finally said. "I'm making dinner."

"Already?"

"Well, I'm practicing."

His brow lifted. "So, you're making it as in…"

My head bobbed. "That's right. Chopping. Mixing. All the hard labor."

He whistled. "Look at you, Rose."

"You're welcome to join us later, if you want. If it tastes horrible, we can order pizza."

The sheriff rocked on his heels, appearing to consider the offer. "I think it's probably best if I decline."

"It's just dinner, Granger," I said. "It doesn't have to mean anything."

He hesitated. "That's the problem, Rose. I'd want it to mean something." He tipped his hat. "Have a good night. I'm sure I'll see you around. I always do."

"Like gum stuck on your shoe," I called after him.

Emotions stirred as I watched him amble back to the patrol car.

He still loves you, Raoul said.

I ignored him and headed into the kitchen. Raoul trailed after me making kissing noises.

"Very mature."

Marley stood at the island with the ingredients lined up in a neat row. "I thought I would get everything ready."

"Thanks."

"It was nice of the sheriff to stop by and thank you. It must be a huge weight off his shoulders." Marley slid the cutting board and knife over to me.

He could've texted, Raoul said.

"Let's make sure we don't kill those herbs," I said. "The next time he stops by, I want to show him they're alive and well." I grabbed an onion and placed it on the cutting board.

"Do you think he might come by more often now?" Marley asked.

I stared at her. "Now what?"

She bit her lip. "Nothing."

"I'm not jumping straight into a new relationship," I said. "I only just got out of one. Besides, I hurt Granger once. I have no intention of making a habit of it."

I didn't miss the glance Marley exchanged with Raoul.

"Don't conspire," I said. "There will be no conspiring in Rose Cottage."

Sheesh. Somebody's paranoid, Raoul said.

"I thought you were Team Alec anyway," I said to Marley.

She fixed her blue eyes on me. "I'm Team Mom. I want whatever…whomever you want."

"Duly noted." I concentrated on the onion on the cutting board and willed myself not to cry.

"You can do it, Mom," Marley urged.

I held the knife the way Arnold Palmer had showed me and started to chop.

I bet I can guess whose head you're picturing as the onion, Raoul said.

"I don't wish Aunt Hyacinth any ill will." In fact, I felt sorry for her. We were hers to lose and lose us she did—in spectacular fashion.

Birthdays will be awkward, Raoul said.

"Everything will be awkward. We'll just have to deal with it." I continued chopping and was pleased that my eyes only burned the slightest bit, not enough to make me stop anyway.

"I think we should invite the cousins to dinner next," Marley said.

"That's a good idea," I said. "It'll be a tight squeeze, but we'll make do."

Does this mean I'll be stuck at the kiddie table? Raoul complained. *Those twins are a nightmare to eat with.* He slid off the counter to the floor.

"Before you go, I have an idea that requires your input," I announced.

Raoul stiffened. *Why do I suddenly feel concerned?*

"I have some money in savings and I've decided we should use it to start a business together."

A pizza business?

"No, nothing to do with food."

Well, that's disappointing.

"I think we should be private investigators."

The raccoon peered at me. *Both of us?*

"Of course. I wouldn't be half as good without my familiar. You'll be my partner in fighting crime."

Raoul tapped his claws together. *And we split the proceeds fifty-fifty?*

"Well, I'll be putting up the capital, so I'm thinking more like seventy-thirty."

Plus pizza day on Fridays?

"I can live with that."

And taco Tuesdays?

"Don't push your luck." I rubbed his furry head. "Someone suggested I think about my skills and decide how I might best utilize them. You and I make a great team and I think we've proven that we can handle the work. Honestly, it won't be much different from my old job. I just don't need to write an article at the end of the case."

Raoul nodded. *Count me in.*

"What about me?" Marley asked.

"You'll assist me when your schedule allows it. School is the priority, though."

Her head bobbed with enthusiasm. "I promise."

I clapped my hands. "This calls for a celebration." I ran to the refrigerator to retrieve a chilled bottle of bucks fizz.

"Could I have some?" Marley asked.

"You can have a sip of mine," I said, popping the cork and filling a flute for me and a bowl for Raoul.

To new beginnings, the raccoon said. He dunked his head in the bowl and the bubbles fizzed around his face.

I held the flute while Marley took a hesitant sip.

She scrunched her nose in disgust. "You really like that?"

"I really do." I emptied the glass in two generous swallows.

My head buzzed with excitement. I'd felt so despondent recently, but now I felt ready to take on the world—or at least, our world in Starry Hollow. As I smiled at Marley and Raoul, my chest filled with so much love, I thought it might crack wide open. I'd been wrong to worry about us. Even if things didn't work out the way we preferred, we would be okay.

I would be okay.

My happiness wasn't dependent on Aunt Hyacinth or Alec or anyone else. It was as it had always been—entirely dependent on me.

* * *

Don't miss book 14, **Magic & Misfortune**!

If you'd like to join my VIP List and receive FREE bonus content, as well as information on sales and new releases, visit www.annabelchase.com.

Printed in Great Britain
by Amazon